Martha's Patience

SALLY BRITTON

Titles By Sally Britton

The Branches of Love Series:

Prequel Novella, *Martha's Patience*

Book #1, *The Social Tutor*

Book #2, *The Gentleman Physician*

Book #3, *His Bluestocking Bride*

Book #4, *The Earl and His Lady*

Book #5, *Miss Devon's Choice*

Book #6, *Courting the Vicar's Daughter*

Other Collections:

The Captain and Miss Winter

An Evening at Almack's: The Heart's Choice

Martha's Patience

Copyright Information

Dedication:
To my best friend, my always and forever.

Chapter One

"If you do not stop this instant, I may have to faint. Or scream. I cannot decide which would have a better effect."

George Brody did not bother to hide his grin at her exasperated tone, though Martha Gilbert whispered the words from behind her fan.

"I mean it, Mr. Brody," she said, dark eyebrows lowered most severely. But the laughter in her green eyes gave her away every time. He knew she found his commentary on the debutantes, surrounding them at a ball hosted by a viscount she'd never actually met, nearly as diverting as he did. Why else would she stand near him, a pace further back from the crowd than most, if not to listen to his wit?

"Miss Gilbert," he responded, lowering his chin and fixing her with narrowed eyes. "If you must do one or the other, I suggest fainting. Screaming will only draw comment on your lack of ability to control your lovely voice, for all can see that you are not in dire circumstances."

She scoffed at him and wrinkled her nose.

"Or you may start a panic. Other ladies could join in the shrieking as they look about for whatever rodent caused your hysteria. But if you faint, I might carry you out to your carriage, which will hasten you home, and then we are finished with this ridiculous evening."

Her smile returned to match the merriment in her eyes, and she closed her fan to smack him on the shoulder with it. Not enough to smart, but he gasped and covered the spot with a hand. "That was not very maidenly of you."

His protest only made her cast her eyes heavenward.

"You are a sore trial to me, Mr. Brody." Martha snapped her fan open again and began to wave it more rapidly.

Though they were only in the first week of February, the ballroom in which they stood was warmer than George liked. There were too many perfumed ladies decked in silk gowns and too many gentlemen wearing wool evening coats. The only relief came from windows on the opposite side of the room, which were cracked open just enough to let the occasional chilly breeze waft inside.

"I doubt such a thing." He waited for her to meet his eyes before he added, "You depend upon me to make nights like these interesting. You would be bored to tears if I weren't here with you."

Her smile faltered and she looked away. "You're probably right."

Despite his teasing, George immediately felt contrite. He ought not to bring up the fact that she remained without a dance partner these last two sets. Having already done his duty in that regard, George could not ask her again, but at least he kept her company.

He did not entirely understand the gentlemen of London. How could they allow Martha, a beautiful young woman, to remain unattached after two whole seasons? This would be the third year she attempted to make a match through London's highest social circles.

"Miss Gilbert, would you like me to bring you some refreshment?" he asked, bending down to speak directly into her ear. He noted the position of a gentleman acquaintance he could bring back with him, giving her another dance partner.

"No, but thank you." Martha smiled again, though it looked more forced than usual. "I think it must be my gown which frightens them away. It is the most unnatural color."

George took up that thread of conversation at once. "Yes. Pink." He shuddered. "Horrid, unpleasant hue that it is, it is no wonder you are stuck here with me."

He well knew that the shade she wore only made the pink in her cheeks appear more charming. It matched the tiny rosebuds she had woven into her hair and made her white gloves and fan stand out, highlighting her delicate wrists and long fingers.

Why would any young lady put feathers, jewels, pearls, or other ridiculous ornaments in her hair when she might be rendered lovelier with fresh flowers? He nearly commented on the buds upon first seeing Martha that evening but decided against it. Given their usual interactions, she might think he jested, and it was hardly a very masculine thing for him to notice.

"Perhaps we could make our way to the windows," she suggested, nodding towards the other side of the room. "Some fresh air would be nice."

"Of course, Miss Gilbert." He bowed and offered her his elbow with as much deference as he would give a duchess. "Your wish is my command."

The twitch of her lips was the only indication she held back whatever humor she felt at his act. Martha wound her arm through his and directed her attention to their path along the outskirts of the dance floor. He matched his pace to her shorter strides and looked down again at the lovely flowers nestled in her dark ringlets before fixing upon her profile.

Why did no man come forward and marry her? He considered her a friend, so he well knew that Martha possessed a remarkable wit, a good intellect, and a pleasant singing voice. George also admitted, albeit only to himself, that her beauty was perfectly obvious.

Was every man in London blind as well as stupid?

"Mr. Brody, why aren't you dancing more with the other wallflowers?" she asked, bringing him out of his thoughts. "I can well see I am not the only one without a partner. As you have already led me through two sets, you might as well help the other poor souls in the room. See there, Miss Whiten. This is only her second ball, and she looks very much at sea."

He looked up at the girl, no more than seventeen if he guessed correctly, standing next to her mother and looking forlorn. "Miss Whiten? I have no objection to dancing with her. It is her mother I fear to approach. The woman could single-handedly retake the American colonies if she put her mind to it. I have no wish for her to put her mind to *me* as a husband for her daughter."

Martha looked up at him, narrowing her eyes in a way that might intimidate a fellow who didn't know her. "Poor Miss Whiten, then. What about Lady Anne?" She nodded to a different corner of the room.

George followed her gaze to the distinguished young woman, daughter of an earl, poised to inherit a large sum of money if she would only marry. "Lady Anne has no wish to dance with anyone untitled. It would only make both of us uncomfortable if I presumed to approach her."

She snorted and covered her mouth with one hand. "I doubt that's true at all. Most ladies find you rather handsome, as you well know."

"Perhaps. But Lady Anne would find an earl or a viscount much handsomer." He puffed out his chest and looked around again. "I could go ask Miss Rachel Candleworth."

Martha's eyes made the quick glance around the ballroom, settling at last on a lovely young woman who sat next to her chaperone, watching the dancing couples with bright eyes. Her hand on his arm tightened a moment, but then she relaxed and nodded.

"Yes, Miss Rachel would enjoy a dance. I am surprised she is not already upon her feet."

"Let me secure you to another friend before I do your bidding and stand up with her." He smiled his most charming smile and looked around until he spotted Lady Littleton, the wife of a baron who lived in their county. "Ah, come." He took Martha directly to her.

Lady Littleton, a fine woman with children several years younger than Martha, greeted them graciously and engaged Martha in conversation at once.

George excused himself and turned away with a barely repressed sigh. He did not truly wish to dance with Miss Rachel, lovely as she may be, because her conversation never drifted far from the weather or how fine a place London was. But what could he expect from someone in her second season? Yet he would not let a young lady who wished to dance, and who was somewhat pleasant company, become a wallflower.

It pained him that Martha Gilbert sat out as often as she did.

He fixed a pleasant expression on his face as he approached the young woman, and when she saw he came for her, she blushed and stood. In moments they were joining the next set, and George told himself he did the right thing, and he tried to enjoy the set.

Martha returned home late that evening, dropped at the doorstep of her family's townhouse by her friends. Her mother had not been feeling well enough to attend but made certain her daughter would not miss the ball. Indeed, Martha's mother kept their social calendar packed with events to the point that Martha was surprised it had taken this long to exhaust the older woman.

Mrs. Gilbert, a cheerful and kind soul, had very delicate health. An abrupt change in the weather often brought on coughs and headaches, and too many nights without enough sleep left her more tired than most. As a young child, she had suffered through many illnesses, and they weakened her constitution considerably.

Norton, their town butler, surprised her when he informed Martha both Mother and Father waited for her in the library.

She discarded her wrap and hurried to her father's book room, a cozy room stuffed with books and comfortable furniture. In some homes, she knew, libraries were only for show. But here, in their house, theirs was a well-loved sanctuary.

On the couch, seated close to one another, her parents sat before a warm fire. Her father's voice carried to the doorway as he read.

"'When I said I would die a bachelor, I did not think I should live till I were married.'" She recognized the line from Shakespeare's *Much Ado About Nothing*.

Her mother chuckled, and Martha took that moment to interrupt the cozy picture they made. She cleared her throat and came further into the room. "Good evening," she said, both parents turning to face her. "I did not think you would wait up this late."

Her father stood and waved her in toward the chair nearest the fire. "Why would we go to bed when we can now ply you with questions about your evening?" he asked, raising his eyebrows high and opening his hands. "All the details are still fresh just now, unmuddled by sleep."

"Oh, Harold. Do not tease her." Her mother tsked at her husband and then turned her attention to Martha. "I wanted to be sure you came home safe and happy. I am sorry I could not attend with you tonight, darling."

"Mama, the Driscolls took very good care of me, as promised." Martha stretched her legs as far as she could before settling into a more ladylike position. "But since we are all here and awake, what would you like to know of the evening?"

Her parents exchanged one of their knowing looks before the questions began.

"Did you dance often?"

"Was there anyone there of note?"

"Any of our friends?"

"Did you meet anyone new?"

Martha laughed and held her hands up. "Dear Papa and Mama, one question at a time."

"Just tell us the whole of it, and we've no need for questions," her father said, reaching to hold her mother's hand, settling deeper into the cushions. Obviously, he meant for the conversation to take some time. She hated to disappoint him.

"There is not much to tell," Martha said, lowering her gaze to the floral carpet. "I danced a few times, with the usual young gentlemen. No one especially stands out." That was a small lie. Mr. George Brody always stood out in her mind. But she could hardly admit to that, not when she had no hopes of him ever realizing it. "Lady Littleton was there, and we spoke for a time. Miss Rachel Candleworth was there with a chaperone." And how much she wished Rachel had remained at home! "But it was not an evening of much note."

She dared to glance up, knowing the looks she would see, yet needing to confirm them. Her mother looked as though her heart pained her, and her father looked perplexed. They would both be disappointed if this, her third season, went by without any offers of marriage.

During her first season, there had been three gentlemen callers, two of which made offers. She declined both, her father allowing it without question, and returned home. Her second season, there were four attentive young men, but she was able to dissuade three of them before they could even think to ask for her hand, and the fourth sought her approval before her father's. She thanked him but declined the offer. Now, her third season upon her, she had not attracted any *beaux*, only the usual callers after a night of dancing. Nothing serious, no one permanent.

But did her parents yet guess that Martha sabotaged herself?

"I am sorry, Martha," her mother said, rising from her seat to come put her hand on Martha's shoulder. "We will not give up, darling girl, until we have found you a loving husband. I promise."

Guilt smote her, and Martha had to look away from her mother's warm smile. Not many young women were as fortunate as she, with parents who wanted her to find love instead of an important connection. Her parents were permitted to make a love match, more than twenty years previous, when such marriages were still rare. They wanted that same experience, a true love story, for each of their three children. Even if it meant sponsoring Martha through a dozen London seasons. Her parents would never censure her for the expense, but Martha knew each season came at a high financial cost.

"Indeed. I think I will go to my club tomorrow and find out if there are any promising gentlemen we have overlooked," her father said, leaning back in his seat and offering her a gentle, teasing smile. "He is out there somewhere."

Martha knew precisely where George Brody resided. His apartments, bachelor quarters, were not so far from their house. He leased the same small house every year. He started coming to London before she did, but took out his lease the same year of her come out. At the time, Martha hoped this meant he had grown up enough that he might pay her some attention.

"Thank you both," Martha told her parents, rising to embrace her mother. "But I am very tired, and I know you need your rest, too. Especially if you are going to scour London in search of a husband for me." She went to her father, and he rose to give her a kiss on the cheek. "Good night, Papa. Mama."

"Good night," they said together, and she went from the room, casting them a last smile over her shoulder before closing the door.

Once in the darkened hallway, Martha allowed her shoulders to fall and her head to droop. Knowing what she had to do, and following through with it, were two very different things. Martha had decided, before coming to London, that if Mr. Brody paid no more attention to her than he had the previous two years, she would give him up entirely.

But, she had reasoned, one ball was not enough of a trial period. She stretched out the experiment to a few social calls, one tea, an assembly, and now was on her third ball where he attended as well. Oh, her hopes rose with each meeting, only to be dashed at her feet before he took his leave of her, every single time.

George would always seek her out, a ready smile on his lips, greet her kindly, dance with her or stand by her side while she conversed with others. But he never acted with any true deference towards her. Honestly, she did not understand him. George could spend an hour at her side, talking and teasing, making her laugh, or engaging her in earnest conversation. But he always walked away with no more feeling between them than before.

Her very first foray into London society, George had been there. He had asked her to dance, never suspecting how her young, lovesick heart raced at the suggestion. Then he proceeded to tell her how ridiculous the ladies of London were, how much he detested the social whirl of the season, and how he needed more sensible people to speak to at each dreaded event his mother forced him to attend.

In her innocence, she offered herself as a willing conversant. In return, he promised to always dance with her at every ball, and keep her company when she wished it.

And where did that leave her now?

"Nowhere," she muttered out loud.

"What was that, miss?" her maid, Beth, asked. The young woman had frozen, halfway out the door when Martha spoke her thoughts.

"Oh. Nothing, Beth. Thank you." She sighed and waited for the door to close before dropping her face into her hands and groaning. She could feel the heat of her cheeks against her palms and knew her blush must be horrid.

"Nowhere. Nothing. That is all I have to show for every second I spend with George Brody." She looked up into her mirror, shooting an accusing glare at her reflection. "Why can't I just move on? Give up on George and try to fall in love with someone else?"

But her heart ached at the very suggestion of such a betrayal.

Martha took one of the rosebuds from the table and twirled it in her fingers, thinking on their shared dances, wishing it meant as much to George as it did to her.

"Tomorrow, I will have to form a new plan. I cannot give up so easily." She kissed the pink rosebud and left it on the table, going to her bed with a much more determined frame of mind.

Chapter Two

The morning calls Martha and her mother accepted were the usual sort, consisting mostly of Mrs. Gilbert's friends. They came to make certain she was feeling better, several even gifting her specially made tea packets, flowers, lemons, and anything they could contrive to bring a smile to her face. Anyone who knew her mother adored Mrs. Gilbert, counting her as a special friend.

George arrived in the middle of the time set aside for visitors, a bouquet of flowers in his arms. He bestowed these on Mrs. Gilbert before taking a seat.

Martha served him a small dish of biscuits and a cup of coffee, as was his preference. Did he even realize she did not have to ask him how to prepare it, or which treats were his favorites? Having seen him in this very room, several times a week, all season long, Martha knew a great deal about his mannerisms and conversational habits.

However, Martha did not expect her mother's first choice of conversation on this particular day.

"Mr. Brody, will you please tell me if you have any friends you are keeping hidden from us?"

George paused, his cup nearly to his mouth, and Martha gasped out loud.

"Mama, please. Do not tease Mr. Brody." She turned wide eyes to George and hoped he could not see the blush she felt in her cheeks. "How is the weather outside, Mr. Brody? We have not yet ventured out."

Mrs. Gilbert would not be dissuaded. She actually laughed. "Oh, Martha. Do not take on so. Mr. Brody is a dear friend of the family. I respect his tastes. Perhaps he has a friend or two we have yet to meet."

Martha had never seen her mother take on a subject with such forthrightness, at least not in a public manner. She stared at the woman who raised her, trying to signal with her wide eyes and a small shake of the head that she did not wish this topic pursued. But perhaps her mother was more ill than she let on, for surely nothing else could explain her determined manner on the topic of her choice.

"You see, Mr. Brody, we have looked a great deal of society over and feel there must be more to it. Martha did not enjoy last evening as she should. Truly, every young lady ought to come home from a ball with excitement over the evening. But my daughter has not found this to be true for her this season."

To her mortification, George began to nod. "I understand you completely, Mrs. Gilbert. I thought the same thing myself. Miss Gilbert is a charming lady, and gentlemen ought to be lined up to ask for the pleasure of dancing with her. I will make it my personal mission to find more astute fellows to introduce into your acquaintance."

"That really is not necessary," Martha managed at last, her voice sounding tight, matching the muscles in her jaw and hands. "The evening went perfectly well. There was merely a shortage of dance partners. I am certain things will improve at the next ball."

Of course, if she encouraged the young men who actually made eye contact with her, instead of immediately returning her gaze to George every time, they might actually *ask* her to dance. Indeed, if she left George behind altogether, there was a good chance she would be deemed more approachable. But Martha had chosen to stand with George, time and time again, rather than seek out the attentions of other gentlemen.

"We will see. But it cannot hurt to have Mr. Brody on the lookout," her mother said, giving her hand a gentle pat.

George did not stay long. When he rose to leave, Martha stood to show him to the door, as was their habit. They usually walked slowly from the little parlor to the front entry, talking of their plans for the day.

Martha decided, by the time it took her to cross from the couch to the doorway, that if her mother could be forthright and daring, then so too could she. "I wonder, Mr. Brody, if we might go for a ride tomorrow in your curricle?" Inviting herself for an outing felt incredibly bold.

But George seemingly thought nothing of it. "Of course. At the fashionable hour?"

She shuddered. "Heavens, no. In the morning, I should think, so we might actually enjoy moving instead of inching through the park."

"That will be most enjoyable. I look forward to it." He bowed, accepted his hat and coat from the butler, and went on his way.

Martha released a breath she had been holding since the moment he agreed to her idea. Norton raised his eyebrow at her, but she only grinned cheekily back.

It was high time Martha did more than sit and wait for George to notice her, and the plan forming in her mind struck her as one she ought to have thought of before.

If George would not notice her on his own, she would *force* him to do so, by whatever means necessary.

George arrived at nine o'clock the next morning, his curricle a light and sporting model he felt rather proud to own. His gray geldings, bred for speed and style, pulled for him today. He did not keep more than three horses in town, as there was little use for more. When he pulled to a stop in front of the Gilbert home, fifteen-year-old Thomas Gilbert waited on the step.

"Ah, hello Thomas," George called, climbing down from the rig. "A bit cold for sitting on the stoop, isn't it?"

Thomas had already risen and come forward, eyes alight, taking in George's horses. "I wanted to see your new animals. Martha said they're real champions. Are they fast?"

George grinned and held the reins out to Thomas. Everyone who knew the family knew that the boy was absolutely mad about horses. If Thomas could, he likely would make his home in the stables with them.

"They've won a fair share of races down Rotten Row. Why don't I take you out tomorrow morning, before the park is too crowded?"

Thomas's eyes grew wider, and he nodded at once. "I'll ask my father."

"Excellent lad." George gave him a pat on the shoulder and went up the steps to collect Martha. He had only to knock before the door swung open.

Martha stood just inside, wearing a smart little green riding suit and coat, complete with a furry white muff and a warm-looking scarf and bonnet. The color of her coat made her eyes stand out against her fair skin.

"Good morning, Mr. Brody," she said, chin tilted down and eyelashes fluttering.

Perhaps the sunlight was overly bright.

"Good morning, Miss Gilbert." He bowed and extended his hand, which she took with a giggle. Strange. While Martha was the soul of good-humor, she rarely giggled over nothing. "Are you ready for our ride?"

"Yes, of course." She put her hand through his arm for the short walk down the steps.

Thomas began chattering about the horse, asking questions, distracting George enough that he put Martha's odd behavior out of his mind for a time.

"Thomas, I promise I will tell you all about Fisticuffs and Bruiser tomorrow morning, but now I must keep my appointment with your sister," he said at last, taking the reins back from the boy.

"Oh." Thomas blinked towards the curricle as if only then realizing Martha sat waiting. "Have a good time, Mr. Brody. Martha." He stepped back, eyes still on the horse, while George climbed back inside.

"Certain you're up for this?" he asked, pulling the lap blanket up and over them both. "It's a bit nippy out."

"I think I will stay warm enough," she answered, scooting just an inch or two closer to his side.

George checked the blanket again, concerned he had not given her enough if she felt she must move toward him. But there seemed ample cloth on her side of the seat. He shrugged and set his mind on the horses. "Walk on," he commanded with a slight flick of the leads.

"Thank you ever so much for the outing today, Mr. Brody." Martha's speech seemed unlike her; her voice was softer, airier than normal. He glanced down at her to see her eyelashes fluttering at him again. "I had positively nothing else to do today, and spending an hour with you in the park will be diverting."

Strange. Not only had her voice changed, but so too had her usual intelligent speech patterns. Martha spoke slowly, most often, her words and tone modulated in such a way that one knew she gave a great deal of thought to each word uttered. He liked that about her—she took the time to speak of things that mattered instead of blurting inane comments like the other young ladies spouted.

"Happy to be of service," he said, still puzzling over this abrupt change in demeanor. "I think the cool air will do us both a great deal of good after the near suffocation we experienced in the ballrooms."

Martha removed a hand from her muff and brought it to her lips, covering a tiny smile. "Oh, I do enjoy being out of doors. But the balls are not all bad. You enjoy the dancing, do you not?" She turned more towards him and leaned a little forward. "You are such a wonderful partner, after all."

George narrowed his eyes, first at her, then at the road before them, turning into the park. "You know how I feel about dancing. It is better than standing about, doing nothing. But it's primarily an activity for the ladies to enjoy."

She nodded the whole time he spoke, her eyes glittering up at him, and he thought she might have come back to her senses at her ready agreement. But her next words dashed that hope.

"Poor Mr. Brody, of course it is not your favorite thing to do, even if you do it well. You would much rather be riding about your fields at home. But of course, you ride very finely, too." She tipped her head to one side and her tiny, false smile returned. "Perhaps when we return home, after the season, you might show me more of your land, tell me of your plans for your farms this year."

His shoulders tightened, and he had to swiftly divert his attention back to the horses.

Has she lost her wits?

Martha had ridden from one side of his land to the other, as their mothers were dear friends, and that meant she was often upon his property. Had he not given her a very thorough tour of the whole thing but two summers past? And did he not speak frequently of his plans with her? She knew very well he had no inclination to marry, at least not until the right sort of woman crossed his path. He wasn't entirely sure what such a woman might be like, but he felt certain he would know her when he met her.

Wouldn't he?

"Will you leave London for spring planting this year?" she asked, bringing him out of his thoughts and back to their unusual exchange.

"Yes. Like every year." He looked at her askance, his hands tightening on the reins. "What about you? Will your family stay the whole of the season?"

Was this what they had come to? *Small talk?*

"Father will return for spring planting, but Mother and I will remain here until the bitter end." Some of her former cadence returned at the end of that phrase. She released a long sigh and turned away from him, facing forward again. "We must enjoy every moment while we can."

That sounded a touch dire.

"While you can?" he repeated, curious, and watching her from the corner of his eye.

Her spine stiffened, and her strange expression—all pleasant politeness—returned, along with that infuriating and insipid manner of speech.

"Why would anyone wish to leave London when there are so many friends to be had, parties to attend, and balls at which to dance? I intend to make the most of every day and night in London." She brought a hand out of the muff to lay on his arm, leaning towards him again. "You will be missed when you return home."

At last, it occurred to George what his friend attempted with her odd conversation and fluttering of hands and eyelashes.

"Good heavens, Martha," he said, quite forgetting propriety demanded a more formal address. "Are you *flirting* with me?"

Her fair skin drained of color, her jaw dropped open, and her eyes widened, then she yanked her hand away from him, stuffing it into her muff with haste. "Flirting? With *you*?" She slid as far away from him as the seat would allow and kept her eyes fixed ahead. "The very idea, Mr. Brody. What a thing to say."

He turned to study her, watching as the white of her skin gave way to a blooming, rose-colored blush. Martha's whole body remained stiff, every inch of her angled as much away from him as possible, given the confines of the curricle. She tilted her chin higher under his inspection and narrowed her eyes, glaring at the trail before them.

"I never would have thought you capable of those artless feminine tricks," he said at last, his frustration mounting. He focused his gaze back on the horses, devoting his mind to the task of driving and trying to unclench his jaw.

What the devil is she thinking? he asked himself, pressing his lips together to avoid saying such a thing out loud.

They were *friends*. They had been since their first season together in London. She the shy, retiring debutante in need of someone to show her the way in society, and he the self-assured, independent young man ready to share the more amusing aspects of the season with someone who needed his guidance. It had all been very clear that first year and then the second, when he introduced her around to all his friends, escorted her to balls and concerts, and made certain she felt comfortable.

Would she undo all their work, their friendship, their trust? She knew him better than that—knew he would not indulge in frivolous flirtation, as he would not pretend at affection.

He darted a quick glance at her to see her posture no longer stiff and proper. Martha's shoulders were slumped, her eyes downcast, and she was biting her bottom lip.

George hoped she wasn't about to cry.

"I am perfectly capable," she said in a manner which he barely heard, "of feminine tricks."

"I've never seen evidence of that," he argued, then snapped his mouth closed, shaking his head. "What's come over you? I know it's your third season, but that's no reason—"

"My third season?" she interrupted, raising her face to look at him, her eyes wide. "You think I must be desperate at this point, do you? Well, I would have to be, to even consider *flirting* with someone like *you*, so disinterested in the very idea of me as a woman as to doubt me capable of being *feminine."*

George's mind scrambled to keep up with her words, and he belatedly realized she had turned the tables on him, changing his surprise into guilt over her wounded pride. How did women do such things?

"That is not what I meant at all," he said, raising his voice despite himself.

"No?" She scoffed and raised her chin higher, her nostrils flaring. "Then what did you mean?" The dare in her sea green eyes was not lost on him.

But George did not pause to think on what he said. Not long enough.

"I meant that you are on your third season, and that must be a sore point for you, to remain unattached this long without offers. But that doesn't mean you have to throw yourself at every gentleman of your acquaintance."

Her jaw hung open before she released a squeal of a most unpleasant nature. "You think I would throw myself at you? I have known you since my infancy, George Brody, and I am not the least bit interested in throwing anything at you right now, except perhaps my boot. I am not the least bit desperate for gentlemen admirers, and I will have you know that I *have* received offers." She turned away from him again, bringing her muff in tight to her body, pushing her arms into it enough that she must be crossing them.

"Then why are you still unattached?" he dared to ask, thinking he caught her in a falsehood.

"None of your business," she bit out. "Please take me home."

The abrupt change in her attitude, and their afternoon, unsettled him. Though he would much rather have it out with her, and get a satisfying answer to his questions, George took advantage of a turn in the lane and pulled the conveyance around. They were not yet halfway through the park, but it was obvious she wished to be rid of him quickly.

When a lady requested to return home, a gentleman obliged her.

He ground his teeth together and slouched over the reins the whole way, irritated beyond reason with her strange shift in character. Neither one spoke until her house came into view.

"Don't forget," she said icily, "that you promised Thomas you would see him tomorrow. You needn't worry that I will be about, since you find my company distasteful and too *female* at present."

That brought him back into the fray. "I never said I found your company distasteful. But if you are to continue on in this manner, with actions I have never seen from you before, perhaps it would be best if we not see each other for a few days. Not until you can be rational again." He jumped down from the curricle and held his hand out to assist her down.

"Rational?" She paused, standing in the curricle, looking down at him. Her eyes narrowed, and her eyebrows came down. "That is what you say to me? That you do not think I am behaving in a logical, reasonable manner?"

“Not at all.” He held his hand higher, impatient for her to take it.

She finally put her gloved hand in his, holding tightly as she stepped down, but releasing it quickly once both feet were safe upon the ground. Her eyes met his again, and he noted her cheeks were pale once more.

“Perhaps I am more feminine than you ever suspected, Mr. Brody. Is that not what all men say, that a woman must be an irrational creature if she behaves in a way you are unable to explain?” She shook her head. “But I will abide by your wishes. You will not see me again any time soon.” Without another word, she spun and hurried up the stairs and into the house, slamming the door behind her.

George stared after her, wondering how he had become the villain in their argument. And why were they arguing? They never disagreed about anything.

He drove away, still trying to puzzle it out.

Chapter Three

Martha went through the rest of her day and evening in a state of irritation. Her father and mother, after receiving a series of curt replies from her at the supper table, did not look into the matter. Thomas attempted to ask her all manner of questions about Mr. Brody's horses, but she put him off with nothing more than a glare.

She withdrew to her room earlier than usual, pleading a headache, and no one protested when she left. Martha knew her attitude ought not to impact her family, who were innocent bystanders, but she did not feel up to pretending any cheerfulness. Not when she had successfully ruined a very good friendship in one short ride.

Beth helped her to bed and left her with a burning candle and a compress for her forehead. Then the maid returned with a teapot and a little cup. "Your mother sent this," she said in a whisper, "for your headache."

Martha's contrite "thank you" broke the spell of her foul temper. Once the door shut on her maid, she relaxed her hold on her emotions, and the tears immediately began falling.

"I've ruined everything," she whispered to the darkened room.

George had every right to be angry with her, she knew. But when he accused her of flirting, which she had been attempting, albeit poorly, all she could think to do was defend herself. The best defense, in her humiliated state of mind, was a good offense.

It did hurt that he did not believe her to be feminine. Even if he meant something else by the word. How could he not see her most gentle qualities? Her love of flowers, music, and dancing? Did he not think her graceful in her movements and voice? Had he not praised her artistry with watercolors and her fine stitches when she gave him new handkerchiefs but two Christmases ago?

Martha knew she could not be held up as the ideal woman, not by all of society's standards, but she did have talent and grace. She worked hard to be kind and gracious, to behave as a lady ought to behave.

But George never saw it. That was obvious now. He did not recognize her accomplishments as worthwhile or attractive. Perhaps her skills in those areas only served to make her blend in with the rest of the misses in London.

She took in a shuddering breath and raised a hand to her pounding temples. The pretended headache became very real as she forced away tears. Martha pushed herself up in bed and took up the teacup, sipping at the herbal brew she knew her mother must have prepared personally for her.

Martha had entertained some notion, before the carriage ride, of simply being more forward with George. Perhaps, if she flirted a tad, he might recognize her feelings for him. But in her nervousness, she botched the whole thing to the point that she had offended him, broken his trust in their friendship, and said horrid things.

How could she ever repair the damage she wrought?

Having George as a friend, if he would not be more, was important to her.

It took a great deal of time, and several more cups of tea, for Martha to fall into a fitful sleep. She determined she must right things as soon as possible. As soon as George would see her again.

Thomas fairly bounced down the steps and leaped into the curricle when George came to give him a ride through the park. The boy barely managed to speak the usual courteous phrases of "good morning" and "thank you" before asking a list of questions about the gray geldings. George's attention became so taken up in answering them that he nearly forgot his irritation with Martha.

Nearly.

George had spent most of the previous evening trying to ascertain why she would put on such a ridiculous front with him. Did she not know they were friends, first and foremost? He knew her better than to fall for either her flirtatious facade or the vehement denials of her purpose in such behavior. Martha *had* meant to flirt with him. But he could not understand why. She knew he had no interest in marriage at present. He'd told her precisely that many times this season. He was only twenty-six. He had plenty of time to find a bride, and he meant to find the right one.

Perhaps she meant to practice upon him? But if that was how she attempted to catch a husband, she went about it the wrong way. Any gentleman of intelligence would prefer her true self to the simpering attitude and affectations of the usual society ladies.

But she said there had been offers for her hand.

That statement at least sounded true.

"Thomas," he said when the boy paused for breath. "I have an odd sort of question for you."

"Yes, Mr. Brody?" the boy asked, sitting straight and looking George in the eye. "About horses?"

George chuckled. "No, not about horses. About your sister."

Thomas frowned. "Martha or Sarah?"

"Martha." George shook his head and sighed. "Why would I ask about a ten-year-old?"

Thomas shrugged. "I don't know. Why would you ask about Martha? She's your friend, isn't she?"

"Yes." George hoped that was still true. "But it is a subject a gentleman doesn't usually discuss with a lady. Not directly. He usually applies to her male relatives."

"Oh." Thomas blinked and sat back. "But doesn't the gentleman usually ask the father if he wants to court a girl?" He crossed his arms and raised his eyebrows, looking intrigued. "You want to court her, right?"

This was not going well. George groaned and regretted bringing up the subject at all. “No, I do *not*. I wanted to ask if anyone else has been courting her. Now or when she’s come to London before.”

This did not seem to impress the boy, as he only shrugged and fixed his eyes on a fine pair of chestnut mares pacing them opposite on the path. Once the horses were gone, he looked back at George. “You want to know if Martha is sweet on anyone?”

George rolled his eyes heavenward. “Yes. If anyone has ever courted her or asked for her hand. That is what I want to know.”

“Those are two different things,” the boy said wisely. “Maybe if you let me drive through the park once, I could give you a good answer.” He grinned like a scamp and held his gloved hands out for the leads.

“That is an interesting proposition,” George said, pretending to think it over. He’d planned to let Thomas drive anyway, but perhaps the boy had grown impatient with him. “Very well. We have an agreement. Talk while you drive.”

Thomas took the reins and controlled the animals with ease, obviously well able to drive a team if he wished. His knowledge of horses extended to the practical readily enough, George knew, and he wondered what Thomas would do with his infatuation of the beasts. That would be a topic for another time, however.

“Start talking, Thomas,” he reminded the boy, sitting back and folding his arms, keeping his eyes on the road ahead in case his assistance was needed.

"Martha's had a few callers this season," Thomas said, "but she doesn't talk about anyone special. Last year, there were four dandies who were always around. Martha wasn't really interested in any of them, but my mother hoped one would be the right man. Her first year, there were more, I think. I don't know, exactly, because they don't really tell me. I just overhear things." He shrugged and pulled the horse around to go down a less-used path at a slightly faster clip. "I'm not supposed to know anything. But I like my sister. She's a good sort of person, as girls go, even if she is bossy."

George's lips twitched, amused by the boy's assessment for all that it had proved unhelpful. What would a youth be told about his older sister's courtships? Precious little, unless one led to something of greater significance.

"I don't think she's in a hurry to get married," Thomas finally added, interrupting George's thoughts. "I think she's just worried she might not find the right person." The boy's ears turned pink at the end of that sentence and he cleared his throat.

"Someday, you'll want to talk about these sort of things, Thomas," George told him. "But I'll let you off for now. You've years yet before you must worry over love and ladies."

"A lot of years," Thomas muttered. "Horses are easier to understand than girls are, in my opinion."

"Very true, lad." George chuckled, but with little humor. "Very true."

When George and Thomas returned to the Gilbert townhouse, Martha flung the front door open and hurried down the steps, not even dressed for the weather. "Mr. Brody," she called out before her brother had stepped down from the conveyance. "Please, might I have a word?"

It would be well within his rights to ignore her or bid her good day, after their last parting words. But George did himself credit and only nodded before coming down from the curricle behind Thomas.

Thomas looked from George to Martha, his eyebrows raised. He sighed. "Thank you for the ride, Mr. Brody." As he walked by Martha on the stairs, she heard him muttering. "Horses are much, much easier."

Ignoring her younger brother, Martha took another step down, bringing her eyelevel with George where he stood on the walkway. She took his measure carefully, hoping he would be open to her apology. He stood with legs apart, hands behind his back, leaning slightly forward.

"What can I do for you, Miss Gilbert?" he asked, his tone completely formal, his face a mask of civility.

She bit her lip and looked down, gathering her words and her courage before speaking.

"I am afraid I must ask a great deal. I must ask for your forgiveness." She looked up, meeting his eyes. "You were right. I behaved in a highly irrational and unfriendly way yesterday. I am sorry for that, Mr. Brody, and I hope that we can be friends once more."

George regarded her quietly, his eyes searching hers, before a smile twitched at his lips. "I cannot stay upset with you, Miss Gilbert. I believe we both said regrettable things. I will forgive you if you will forgive me. As to our friendship, nothing will ever change that, not even the occasional disagreement."

Martha's relief was bittersweet. They would go back to how they were, before her ridiculous experiment, and he would see her only as the little neighbor girl in need of a dance partner. But she would take what she could get, even if all he offered was friendship.

But another hard truth had come to her in the night. If George could only be her friend, she must give up her love for him and try to find another who would return her feelings, or else remain alone.

"Thank you, Mr. Brody." She took one step back. "Would you care to come inside for some breakfast? It is still obscenely early for being out, you know."

His familiar grin appeared, and he stepped up beside her, offering his arm. "You know I would never turn down breakfast."

She smiled, but the pleasure of his company was tempered by the pain of knowing she must let him go.

Chapter Four

When George went to meet Martha and her mother at the next ball, he hoped they would be back on even footing again. Three days had passed since Martha's apology, and they had not been in one another's company since.

It took some time to locate the Gilbert ladies. The ball must have pleased the organizers a great deal, as the turnout made it easy to label the event a "crush." The crowds in the public rooms made getting to the ballroom difficult, but George managed it at last.

The first thing he saw upon entering was Martha, in the midst of a lively reel one would normally consider too jaunty for a London ball. But there she was, arm-in-arm with a gentleman George could vaguely recall meeting once, smiling brightly and looking as though she had never enjoyed a dance more.

George watched, trying to place the fellow, and he saw the man's eyes turn to follow her, even when the dance did not call for such strict attention. Whoever he was, he certainly admired Martha quite openly.

Which made George frown.

Who was that man, to make Martha look that happy? There was nothing special about the dance, so it must be the partner who gave her such enjoyment.

His eyes sought out her mother next. Mrs. Gilbert would offer an explanation of things, he knew. He waded through the crowded edges of the dance floor to the chairs and felt it a lucky thing to find one unoccupied beside Martha's mother. He sat down abruptly, without invitation, causing her to start.

"Oh, Mr. Brody, it's you. Good evening."

"Good evening, Mrs. Gilbert." He smiled and inclined his head. "How are you feeling today?"

"I am much better, thank you. It's a good thing, too." She gestured toward the dancing couple with her hands. "We have been here an hour, and Martha has not sat down once. Every time a dance ends, I make an introduction, and she is swept away at once." George could not fault her the proud smile she wore, or the excited gleam in her eye. Every mother in London experienced pressure to marry off their daughters, in one way or another, and for a girl to be this successful in an evening would be a thrilling achievement.

"Wonderful," he said at last when he realized she was waiting for a response. "I am glad she is enjoying herself. I will simply have to wait for my turn then, won't I?" He sat straighter and looked back to where Martha now moved down the line, hand-in-hand with her partner. "But who is the fellow she's dancing with?"

"Oh, that is Mr. Simms. He is the second son of Lord Simms, the Baron of Burdess. Isn't he a marvelous dancer?" Her bright tone very nearly grated on his nerves. If he did not like Mrs. Gilbert so much, he might have winced.

"Ah. Yes. He goes to my club." George tilted his head to one side. "But you said Miss Gilbert has been dancing the last hour? Who else has had the pleasure of her hand?"

Mrs. Gilbert gave him two more names, both of which were respectable and known to him. But he could not recall either of those gentlemen showing any interest in Martha before, and he knew they had all been at other balls and events at the same time. Mrs. Gilbert showed no inclination to worry over that fact, so he must keep his thoughts to himself.

The set ended what felt like an eternity later, on the arm of her dance partner, Martha came back to her mother. The gentleman bowed to Mrs. Gilbert.

"Thank you, ma'am, for your daughter's company. She is an excellent dancer."

Mrs. Gilbert nodded, almost regally.

George was on his feet and bowing to Martha the moment the other gentleman released her. "Miss Gilbert, may I have this dance?"

Her smile faltered. "Oh, I am sorry, Mr. Brody. The next two are promised. Would you like me to save you the third?"

He ought not to have been surprised, given her apparent success this evening, but Martha had never declined an offer to dance with him before. "Yes. Please."

"Miss Alice Trilby is just over there, and she has not danced more than once." Martha pointed towards the young woman she named, and he looked, but without much interest. "If you wish to dance, I am certain she would be very happy to be asked."

Then her next partner appeared and whisked her away before she could say another word.

Mrs. Gilbert rose from her chair and came to stand next to him, watching as couples took their places on the floor. He felt her eyes turn to him, and he tried to smile.

"Your daughter will be exhausted if this keeps up," he said lightly.

"I do hope so. She loves to dance, and there is not a better feeling than to be worn out from a ball." Mrs. Gilbert chuckled and gave him a pat on the arm. "You had better go dance with Miss Alice if you wish to be a true gentleman."

He nodded and went to ask the lady in question, though he could hardly give her the attention she deserved as they moved across the floor. His eyes kept going down the line to Martha, watching as she threw herself into the enjoyment of the evening. For some reason, try as he might to be happy for her, George could only feel disappointed that he had not arrived to dance with her sooner.

Martha's exhaustion kept her abed later than usual, and her feet still ached when she finally went down to a late breakfast. Her mother looked as though she had only just arrived at the table as well, buttering a scone and yawning delicately into her wrist. Though she at times took breakfast in her rooms, this season she almost always appeared at the table after a ball, the better to discuss any developments with Martha.

"Good morning, darling," her mother greeted. "I'm afraid your father and brother have devoured all the bacon, but there are still pastries and some cold ham."

Martha murmured her thanks and went to the sideboard to put together a small plate of food.

"Wasn't that a splendid evening, Martha? Perfectly wonderful. You never sat out, not one dance. I am looking forward to our morning calls today, to see who comes in person and who sends flowers." Mrs. Gilbert clapped her hands together, her eyes sparkling despite the late hours kept. "This was always my favorite part, you know. I loved the dancing, but then having a more personal exchange with a gentleman kept me in a state of complete distraction."

But Martha could only force a smile and nod, unable to tell her mother she felt the same. Truthfully, she only felt worn out, and the idea of sitting through a dozen morning calls did not appeal to her. Though she had firmly decided she could no longer wait on George to take notice of her, she still could not think any of the gentlemen she danced with truly compared to him.

She knew she was being unfair. She hardly knew those gentlemen, whereas her history with George Brody was long and involved many lovely memories.

"Martha? Are you all right?"

Her mother's question brought her back to the moment, and she realized she had been standing with a scone in a pair of tongs for far longer than necessary. She hastily put the treat on her plate and went to her seat.

"I am well enough. Only tired." She lifted a fork and tried to dig into her plate in a manner which would suggest some exuberance, though the cold food was hardly appetizing.

Mrs. Gilbert raised her eyebrows at her daughter and adjusted the shawl on her shoulders. "Martha, what is it? You don't seem very happy about your triumph at the ball last night."

"Perhaps I am only overwhelmed?" Martha winced, hating that it sounded more like a question than a statement. Surely, she ought to know her own mind. "Yes. I am simply going over the evening in my thoughts and sorting out the gentlemen."

A skeptical gleam appeared in her mother's eyes. "Sorting out the gentlemen?"

"Yes." Martha raised a cup of tea to her lips and took a small sip. When her mother continued to stare, she tried to explain further. "Into categories. That I might better keep track of them. Their likes and dislikes."

"Do those things matter, darling?" her mother asked, a frown now accompanying the skepticism.

Obviously, Martha must be making a terrible mess of her explanations. "I think so. I should learn all I can of the gentlemen, or else I might not ever find one I like. And if there are to be many of them, I must categorize them."

"Darling, that doesn't make any sense. You either like someone or you don't. Categorizing a gentleman's preference of book or sport isn't going to aid you when it comes to matters of the heart." Her mother reached out and laid a hand on her arm. "And while love does not always happen all at once, it is something that comes naturally. No list making or sorting necessary."

Martha looked down into her tea. "Oh. Of course." She put the cup down and stared at her plate, trying to decide what to attempt eating next.

"Hm." Her mother gave her hand a pat and turned her attention away, giving Martha leave to relax. She had no wish to disappoint her mother and admit that only one gentleman, and only one dance the night before, had mattered at all to her.

George had his dance with her, but he was not at all in a pleasant mood, judging from his lack of proper conversation and the noticeable absence of his customary wit and smile. Had he not forgiven her after all?

Martha pushed her food around her plate until she felt she had stayed at the table long enough to keep her mother from worrying. Then she excused herself and went to her room, hiding from any further conversation about the night before. It might not be entirely fair, given her mother's delight in the subjects of balls and dancing, but Martha had not enjoyed it. Pretending to be happy and pleasant all evening, trying to get to know near-strangers during a dance, had not been as satisfying as she'd hoped.

When the time came for her to descend to the parlor to accept callers, she had to pinch her cheeks to give them color. The only thing lifting her spirits was that George would come. He always did, after a ball, to discuss the evening with her and make their plans for the coming social events. He often arranged his calendar to suit hers, a thing she had always hoped would come to mean more.

Martha sat through three gentlemen and had received four bouquets by the time George arrived at the door. Thankfully, it was after other guests had left, and she need not divide her attention between him and another.

"My, look at all the flowers," he said upon entering the room, where most of the bouquets were on display in the corners. "You must be popular, Miss Gilbert."

The heat returned to her cheeks, and she hoped some color with it. "Oh, it is only a few gentlemen being polite." She gestured to George's usual chair, the most comfortable one in the room. She knew he preferred it because the legs were sturdy, not ornate and spindly as most fine chairs.

Her mother, sitting at a discreet distance with her sewing, beamed up at George's entry. "Hello, Mr. Brody. I am glad to see you today."

"And I you, Mrs. Gilbert." He went to her and bowed over her hand. "I hope you are doing well after your late night."

"Yes, thank you." She released him and turned her attention back to her sewing. "Go ahead and sit.

I am certain Martha will wish to talk to you of her success."

Martha bit her lip and turned toward the tea tray, making a plate of sweets for George without thinking. "Shall I order your coffee?"

"Yes, thank you."

Their habits during one of his visits only served to remind her how well she knew him, how well suited they would be if he could only love her.

She banished that melancholy thought and brought him the plate with a smile. "You must tell me who you danced with last night, Mr. Brody. I was not able to keep track of you."

He chuckled and rested his plate on his knee. "I don't blame you. How did you keep from getting dizzy, twirling and gamboling from one end of the ballroom to the other? Every time I looked up, there you were, whether it was a minuet or a reel."

Martha relaxed into her seat. He was not vexed with her. Perhaps he had only been tired the previous evening.

"I have never had the opportunity to boast that I danced the night away, and I thought I might like to try it once," she said, keeping her tone light. "I confess, as entertaining as it was, my poor dancing slippers are quite worn out."

"I would imagine so. Were you trod on very often?" he teased, a glint in his eyes that made her laugh.

"Only every other partner."

"That is a mercy if only half were poor dancers. Not everyone is so skilled as myself." He sat up and puffed his chest out importantly, but they both laughed. "Truthfully, if not for your governess coming about and making us learn to dance together at home, I would likely be an appalling partner."

"You complained that whole summer long." She rolled her eyes heavenward and shook her head at him. "Every time we arrived with the dancing instructor, you had to be hunted down. Even though you knew perfectly well that we would come."

He laughed and leaned back in his chair, settling in comfortably as he always did. "Can you blame me? I avoided those lessons for years, and then I was forced into them at twenty. And how old were you? Fourteen? And you always looked at me as if you thought I might bite you."

She calmly sipped her tea. "You certainly looked irritated enough that you might've."

Mrs. Gilbert coughed in a manner that sounded suspiciously like a laugh, causing George and Martha to exchange grins. Though Mrs. Gilbert rarely interjected herself in the young people's conversations, she took as much enjoyment from the exchange as they did.

The coffee arrived, but so did the butler, with a card on a platter.

"A Mr. Bellingford to see you, Miss Gilbert."

"Oh?" She took the card and looked it over, her mind a sudden blank. She thought she recalled the name but could not recollect what he might've looked like. Had they danced? Of course, they had. She had danced with everyone who asked her.

"Bellingford? He's a dandy if I ever saw one."

She suddenly remembered a blazing pink waistcoat. “Oh, thank you, Mr. Brody. I couldn’t recall which one he was.” She looked up at Norton. “I suppose you had better show him in. We danced the minuet, I think. Any man who suffers through that ought to at least be permitted biscuits and tea.”

She turned her attention back to George, whose smile looked rather less cheerful than before. “Don’t you agree, Mr. Brody?”

“Yes. Of course. The minuet.” He cleared his throat and looked down at his plate, only half his sweets eaten. He stood and moved quickly to put the plate back down on the tray and shook his head when she gestured to the coffee. “I’m sorry, but I have just remembered an appointment. Perhaps I might call on you at another time?” He glanced up, but his chin remained lowered.

“Always, Mr. Brody,” she answered, the abrupt change in formality surprising her.

“Splendid. Good day to you, Miss Gilbert. Mrs. Gilbert.”

“Good day, Mr. Brody,” her mother answered.

He left the room with enough haste that he very nearly ran into Mr. Bellingford, who wore a jacket in an alarming shade of green. Martha did not have time to think over George’s hasty departure. She turned her attention quickly to her new guest, but George’s half-full plate and coffee cup served to remind her that at least he had come, however briefly.

Mr. Bellingford launched into his raptures over the entertainment of the previous evening, and Martha attended to him with politeness. But her eyes kept straying to the lonely plate, and consequently her heart continued to pain her. George had gone the moment a suitor appeared. He would not be moved to action by seeing her with another. He did not feel for her as she did for him.

Martha must content herself with the knowledge that he still counted her a friend. She had no other choice.

Chapter Five

George took out a subscription to a library very near his flat, and he often went to make use of it. Though he would not consider himself a scholar, he read with great frequency for both knowledge and entertainment. After he left Martha with her caller, he went straight for the familiar comfort of shelves and tables stuffed with books. He hoped to lose himself between the covers of an adventure or else the philosophical wisdom of the Far East.

But he walked by book after book, barely skimming the titles, not even reaching to lift a volume for closer inspection. George did not realize his lack of attention until he bumped into the wall at the end of a row of books. He stepped back, took in the wall, then looked to the shelves.

What is the matter with me? he asked himself.

Perhaps he was not in the mood to read.

He took himself back out into the cold February air, pulling his coat tighter around him as he went. Before long, he stood inside his own rooms, leased out for the season. His valet had the afternoon off, which left George to see to his own comfort and hang all of his outerwear in the closet.

The flat felt eerily still and silent. Living on his own, as many a young bachelor did at this time of year, usually gave him a sense of freedom and independence. He had no one to please but himself.

A housekeeper came into his home a few times a week, his valet saw to most of his needs, and he ate at his club or a cafe or had supper with friends. Usually, he hadn't the time to sit and notice the quiet.

George put kindling in the fireplace and stoked the embers back into a small blaze of warmth. The cheery sound of the fire crackling lifted his spirits somewhat. He looked around the room until he found the news-sheets from that morning. He settled into his favorite chair, placed perfectly between hearth and the window, and turned his mind to the news of London and England.

Despite the very lengthy articles explaining the procedures now gone through to settle on a new Archbishop of Canterbury, which only that morning had interested him, George found himself rereading the same three sentences over and over without any real comprehension. Disgusted with his lack of attention, George thrust the paper onto a side table and glared out the window to the street below.

Since his visit with Martha Gilbert, he had been out of sorts. He well knew why. Giving up his usual place to allow her dandified gentleman to come calling did not agree with him. George had his habits, and he liked them. It was his custom to sit with the Gilberts many afternoons a week, often longer than what most would consider a polite amount of time to stay, but he never felt unwelcome. Mrs. Gilbert always assured him he was practically family and he could spend all the hours he wished under their roof.

Martha always enjoyed his company. They would talk for above an hour about a book or a play, share their opinions on the newspapers they read, and laugh over the gossip columns. They never ran out of things to say to one another.

But he could hardly stay and monopolize her company when she had gentlemen coming to see her, after a successful night at a ball. Who knew but that one might be the perfect man to make her an offer of marriage? She might even fall in love with one of them. But that would not happen if George were there, eating the best sweets, sitting in the most comfortable chair.

When that silver tray was brought in with a card for Martha, he acted immediately. He would not be the reason she failed in securing a good future. He would not allow his friend to be denied what every maiden wished to find during a London season.

George shoved both hands through his hair and slumped forward in his chair, his elbows on the arms of the chair.

Why did choosing to excuse himself from her home leave him in such a state, if he knew it the right thing to do?

"Because I don't wish to give up time with Martha," he said out loud, the realization shocking him. He pushed himself up from the chair, his entire body electrified as if a bolt of lightning had struck him. "I don't want to give *her* up." George's heart started hammering against his rib cage in a manner it normally reserved for horseback riding.

But if she marries, I give her up for good. He hated the thought, robbing himself of any excitement his earlier realization caused. *A married woman has no business spending time with a bachelor.*

"This will never do," he muttered, lowering his head and tucking his hands behind his back. He paced the length of the room, then turned back to retrace his steps.

I want her to be happy. She wishes to marry. I cannot deny her that wish, not if I am a true and honest friend.

Even thinking about her leaving London on the arm of another man disturbed him. George did not want to imagine it, though he knew if she ended the season unattached it would lower her spirits greatly. How could he keep her as a friend and still see her happily married to another man?

Another man.

The thought stayed with him, his mind enveloping it, turning it over, and then finally realizing what the true problem was with the phrase.

"I don't wish to see her with *another*. I want her to be with me." Saying the words out loud finally gave him the clarity he needed to understand what he must do. "I must court her. I must determine if we will suit one another as more than friends."

His heart lifted, and he very nearly walked out of his flat to go and see her again, straight away, but he stopped himself in time to form a more reasonable plan. If he wanted to court Martha, a dear friend, he would have to go about it right.

She could not mistake his intentions, and he must be certain she would welcome the idea or else risk losing her friendship forever.

Martha thought so long over George's strange behavior at the ball, and then at his morning call, that she gave herself a headache. Truly, she could not understand why he would change his nature as abruptly as he had, unless he was still upset with her over the attempts to flirt with him. But after her apology, she thought they had mended their fences well.

Whatever the matter was, she was quite tired of it. Martha determined she would put George from her mind and enjoy herself more. Consequently, when he next came to call, she had just come down the stairs in her riding habit to meet with a handsome young baron who wanted to go horseback riding in the park. She thought the exercise might lift her spirits more than the tea her mother kept plying her with.

"Good afternoon, Mr. Brody," she said as she descended the steps. "What brings you here this afternoon? It is not your usual visiting hour." Perhaps he did not know how out of character he was behaving.

George smiled up at her, his grin stretching his face in a manner that nearly alarmed her. "I am aware of that, but I have a particular matter I wish to speak to you about."

Martha pushed aside her irritation as best she could when she realized he must have come bearing some news of a scandal. They both laughed over the gossip sheets enough, especially when the "horrifying news" of someone's *faux pas* was overblown to the point of comedy. But she really did not have time to engage with him in such matters.

"We will have to discuss it later, Mr. Brody," she said, as firmly as she knew how. "I have an engagement at present, and I do not wish to keep a gentleman waiting."

George blinked, and she took the last step, bringing her to stand next to him. "Oh? You're dressed for riding." He only just noticed, it seemed. "That is unfortunate. Are you sure you couldn't spare a moment for one of your oldest friends?" He bent his head as he spoke in a manner she found condescending.

"I am afraid, old friend, that you will need to wait your turn." She stepped around him and started walking for the door, knowing her horse would be waiting for her, and perhaps the baron would be ready too.

He caught up with her quickly, his long strides taking him in front of her so he could cut her off. She stopped and looked up at him with a glare. "Really, Mr. Brody. You would not wish a lady to arrive late to an appointment with you. Why would you force another man to do so?"

"Another man." He snorted. "Miss Gilbert, I wish to speak to you very much, and it is important. It is about your search for a husband."

Immediately the heat rose up her neck and into her cheeks.

"Mr. Brody, I thought we had finished discussing such matters? I already told you, I am not desperately seeking a husband. I am enjoying my time in London. I am fortunate enough to have some very fine gentlemen giving me their attention at present, and that is enough. I have no wish to say another word about my private matters to you or anyone else."

Why did he have to continue this subject? He could not know how it hurt her, that he would discuss such things with her in a lighthearted manner, grinning all the while. But surely, he saw that she was through with the subject.

"You don't understand," he continued, raising both hands as if to placate her. "I don't want to talk about them. I wanted to talk about me. About our friendship."

Friendship? She thought with further irritation. *Now he wishes to discuss our friendship, as if that is more important than my season?*

"Mr. Brody," she said quickly, not allowing him to breathe out another word. Each thing he said only served to hurt her more. She did not want his friendship when that was all he would give. Every time he came to her home, appeared in a ballroom, or *smiled* at her, she was only reminded of what she could never have: his love. He would only continue to distract her from other gentlemen who might be willing to share their hearts and lives with her.

"Yes, Miss Gilbert?" he asked, the light in his eyes still bright and absurdly cheerful. He likely thought she would concede and show him into the parlor for a discussion on their *friendship*.

He could not be more wrong. In that instant, Martha knew it was high time for her to protect her heart. No one else ever would.

"I have appreciated your friendship for many years, and I find you to be a very pleasant sort of gentleman overall, but I am afraid I must ask that you no longer come to my home or attend me at events." That smug, happy expression on his face began to melt away. "I am enjoying myself in London. I am not that uncertain little miss who clung to the walls during her first season. I have many gentlemen friends and callers, and you need not worry over me anymore. In fact, I believe it may have been your *friendship* keeping others at bay, all this time."

"Pardon me?" he said, his tone disbelieving. "You are blaming me for *what* exactly?"

"Not exactly blaming you, but as I think on it, I believe it makes perfect sense. Anyone who has seen us together would be likely to form the idea that we spend a great deal of time in each other's company. This could be misconstrued as the two of us having an understanding, or at least taking our time at arriving at one."

Speaking the thoughts out loud, they sounded quite logical. At last, she had the perfect excuse to take a step away from Mr. George Brody and shield her battered heart.

"And since this is my third season, and I would rather not have any further speculation sent my way by other young women and their mothers, I think it best we refrain from seeing any more of each other. Then I might receive more serious consideration from other gentlemen. Now, if you will excuse me." She stepped around him and did not look back. "I do not wish to be late."

She did not look at him, though she wished to see how he took her little speech. But seeing him angry would only make her defensive; seeing him confused would make her wish to stay to drive home the point. And, really, she did not need to spend another moment near him.

It hurt too much.

Martha left the front door of her home, went directly to the mounting block, and was assisted into the saddle by a groom. The baron was waiting for her, and he smiled as he tipped his hat in greeting.

Martha forced a smile. "Shall we, my lord?"

Though she rode towards Hyde Park, she could not keep her heart from aching at leaving George behind.

Chapter Six

Martha did not realize how seriously George would take her words. Not until she attended a card party, a ball, and a supper party where he did not make appearance. Martha knew he'd been invited, as he came to events hosted by each family numerous times in the past. He must have believed her when she dismissed him with such coldness.

She couldn't decide whether that made her happy or melancholic.

When her mother remarked on it one day, after they bid farewell to a particularly attentive caller, Martha bit her lip to keep from blurting out the answer as to his whereabouts.

"I hope he isn't ill," her mother murmured. "I think I'll send one of the footmen around, or a messenger, to ensure he is well. The poor man has no one to look in on him, with his mother staying in the country this season."

"I am certain he is fine," Martha said, righting the tea tray. "He is likely busy with his own affairs. If Mr. Brody needed help of any sort, he would know to send for us."

Mrs. Gilbert pulled her shawl tighter around her, not looking convinced. "Men never ask for help, darling. You ought to learn that now before any of your callers become serious."

"Yes, Mama." Martha sat again and took up her embroidery. "What did you think of Mr. Keller's visit?"

"He is a pleasant gentleman, I suppose. But you were not very impressed by him." She chuckled. "Poor man. I think he was rather taken by you."

"Oh, I don't know." Martha rested her embroidery in her lap. "What about Lord Wilton?"

"You didn't like him either, Martha," her mother stated evenly.

Martha narrowed her eyes. "How do you know that?"

Her mother sighed. "Dear girl, I'm your mother. I notice things. You hardly smiled when either of those men were here. You appeared distracted, most of the time, as though your thoughts were elsewhere. If you were interested in either of those gentlemen, I would have seen it." Her mother shook her head and looked at the clock. "That is what made me think of Mr. Brody. He usually comes around this time of day, and you are always more lively when he is present."

Martha concentrated more firmly on her needle and thread. "It's easy to get along with someone I already know well."

"Mr. Brody is an old friend." Mrs. Gilbert did not speak again for several long minutes, but when Martha refused to say another word and reached for a new spool of thread, her mother spoke again.

"Martha, I cannot help but feel that the season is wearing on you a trifle. You were lively and happy a month ago, but now you look tired. You move about as if you are in a daze. Perhaps I ought to cancel a few of our activities this week."

"Mama, I am perfectly well. I promise. I am little used to being this busy, but it is only good for me. Think of all the new gentlemen we have met." Martha forced the cheer into her voice as she spoke, never meeting her mother's eyes. "I would dislike missing an opportunity to further those acquaintances."

Mrs. Gilbert hummed rather noncommittally before continuing. "I wish we did not sacrifice an old friend for all these near-strangers, none of whom truly hold your interest."

When Martha said nothing, refusing to take the carrot her mother kept dangling before her, her mother continued to fuss with the fringe on her shawl before finally blurting, "Why has that foolish man been away? That's what I would like to know."

It took Martha several seconds before she realized she stared at her mother with her mouth agape. "Mama! Who—You don't mean Mr. Brody?"

"Who else would I mean?" The normally staid and polite woman raised her eyebrows in a most skeptical manner. "What other man of our acquaintance has been scarce of late? But if George Brody is too busy to give you the attention you deserve, perhaps you are better off without him."

"Mr. Brody is a friend," Martha protested. "And he gives me enough attention, as a friend. We should not speak ill of him."

"A friend would not completely abandon you without explanation," her mother countered. "Unless you know something I do not?"

Martha hesitated in her answer. She had never told her mother a falsehood and did not wish to begin now. But how could she phrase it in a way that would placate her mother in regards to George? She had no wish for him to be lowered in her mother's estimation.

"I may have asked him not to come around as much," she finally admitted, seeing no other way around the matter.

Her mother gasped and put a hand over her heart. "You did what to poor Mr. Brody?"

"Mama, you not a moment ago called him a foolish man," Martha reminded her slowly, trying not to smile at the abrupt reversal. "But I had a very frank discussion with him about how he was always present and how that *might* be the reason I did not attract more gentlemen. Obviously, he took me at my word."

"Obviously." Mrs. Brody shook her head and then reached up to massage her temples. "I cannot believe you would do that. Not when you enjoy his company. Not when you like him as much as you do."

"I would much rather find someone to love than spend time with someone who only likes my company on occasion," Martha said, feeling her cheeks grow warm. She stood and dropped her embroidery on the couch, suddenly too agitated to even pretend an interest in it. "And it has changed things. I now have more gentlemen seeking my company than ever before. One of them will be the right one. Eventually."

"Oh dear." Martha turned to see her mother looking increasingly distressed, her mouth turned down in a frown and her face paling. "But, darling, I thought you already had the right one. Truly."

Martha shook her head and released a bitter laugh. "Who would that be, Mama? Every gentleman I have mentioned, you point out that I do not actually like them. And you have been correct, every single time."

"But that is because you love Mr. Brody."

Martha's jaw completely dropped and her cheeks flooded with heat at that declaration. It seemed her mother was full of surprises today.

Martha shook her head in denial but could not help asking, "How did you know?"

"I am your mother, Martha," she stated again. "I know you. I know how you look when you are happy, and you are never so happy as when you are with Mr. Brody. I thought he would certainly offer for you at the end of the first season, and we would have to make him wait, to be sure you both had affection for each other. Then, I was sure it would be during your second season, as you and he were so often in company." Mrs. Gilbert dropped her eyes to the floor, and she shook her head. "This is terrible."

"Mother," Martha said slowly, more formally. "It does not matter how a lady feels for a gentleman if he does not reciprocate her regard. Even if I did love him, he has never loved me back."

Mrs. Gilbert stood and came around the furniture to wrap her arms around her daughter, her embrace warm. "Dear child, I'm sorry. I watched you both for so long, and I thought he would come to see what was so obvious to me. I felt you were meant for each other."

Martha returned the embrace, grateful for the comfort it offered, even though it brought her dangerously close to tears. "I did, too. But Mr. Brody has never indicated he wished for more than friendship. And when I asked him to go, he did. A man in love would not give up so easily." She sniffled and stepped back from her mother. "And it is all right. I will find love. Someday."

"Oh, dear." Her mother pulled a handkerchief from her sleeve and dabbed at the few tears Martha had not been able to hold back. "You are a very brave girl, to stand and smile when you say such sad things. But know that I am here for you, should you need to talk. And if you need to recuperate, allow yourself time to heal, we can forgo a few of the items on our calendar."

"Thank you, Mama. But I think it is best if I pretend all is as it should be. I do not wish to flounder about in my emotions anymore. If you do not mind, I think I ought to practice for Lady Annesbury's concert."

"Brave girl," her mother said again, giving her a gentle pat on the cheek. "Very well, go practice. I will join you shortly. But if anything changes, you tell me at once. I will see to it that you are taken care of, darling."

Martha, relieved of her burden, was grateful that her mother understood.

~~~

George wallowed in his disappointment and heartache for several days. He went nowhere, turned down all invitations, and did not even bother to dress in case anyone came to call. He sat before his fire in his dressing gown and stocking feet, not even allowing his valet to shave him.

He knew he must look wild, but he did not feel it. He did not feel much of anything.

"Mr. Brody," his valet ventured one morning, holding a silver tray stacked with invitations and calling cards. "Your friends are beginning to worry. Have I your leave to answer a few of these notes? I can tell them you are ill and need your rest."

George grunted in response and waved a hand dismissively.

"Very well, sir." His valet hesitated another moment before asking, "Would you like a bath, sir? They always make you feel better."

George raised his eyes to the man and shook his head. "I don't wish to feel better at present, thank you."

"If I might ask," the man continued, swallowing his propriety to do so, "Why are you upset, sir? Are you—that is—has someone died?"

George groaned and shook his head, bending forward to rest it in his hands. "I am not in mourning, Simms. No one has died. I just want to be left alone."
~~~

"Very well, Mr. Brody." The gentlemen's gentleman bowed and left the room, but the silver tray full of invitations remained on a side table.

With nothing better to do, George pried himself from the chair and went to gather the envelopes and cards before returning to his seat. He started with the cards, glancing at names and any notes written on them. If they were of interest, he dropped them into his lap. But most of them ended up being expertly slung into the fire, where they turned brown and crumpled in on themselves in a most satisfying manner.

George went through the invitations next, opening seals roughly, not caring if he wrinkled or tore the paper. Most of those went in the fire, too, especially if he suspected Martha's family of receiving an invitation. He only hesitated once, when his eyes landed upon the seal of the Earl of Annesbury. While he didn't know the earl personally, they lived in the same county, and he'd attended the balls held at the family's country estate. His mother had been good friends with Pamela Calvert, the Countess of Annesbury, for years.

That invitation he would certainly have to attend to.

Simms came back in, carrying a tea tray. "I know you said you wished to remain undisturbed, sir. But as you hardly touched breakfast, I thought I had better leave you something to eat, should you get hungry."

The valet's eyes noticed all the paper turning to ash in the fireplace and he nearly dropped the tray in shock. "Mr. Brody, sir, had I not better send your regrets if you aren't attending those events?"

It was the height of rudeness not to send regrets if one did not accept an invitation, but George didn't care much about that at present. "If you can remember who sent what, you're welcome to try." George stood and held out the invitation from Lord and Lady Annesbury, taking the tray with his other hand. "Respond to this one. Tell them I'll come."

He took the tray with him, back through the rented rooms to his bedroom. He kicked the door shut behind him and put the tray down. He wanted nothing more to do with people today, especially if he must attend a concert on the morrow.

Chances were excellent, he well knew, that not only would the Gilbert family attend, but it was likely Martha had been invited to sing. She had a voice like an angel and, since she was from the same county as the Calverts, they would be happy to put her forward on a night of polite entertainment. Could he manage to sit through listening to her sing, knowing she would wish him far away from her?

His misery before, when he had to share her, was nothing to the heartbreak he felt now when she denied him even that. At first, he had wondered if it was a mercy that she did not hear him proclaim his desire to court her. Perhaps it was for the best, he reasoned, that he not make a complete fool of himself.

After days of doing nothing but thinking, he wished he had declared himself. He wished he told her what she meant to him. The difficulty, truly, was that he hadn't understood it himself until she sent him away.

George realized, hours after arriving home, going over his feelings and her dismissal, that he loved her.

He loved Martha with his whole heart and soul. He did not know when it started, he could not pinpoint a time or place, but George knew it to be true. If he had led with that when he saw her, and given her his feelings the moment he caught sight of her on the stair, would things be different now?

Martha dreamed of a love match; she wanted a deep and abiding devotion, a marriage of heart and mind, as her parents had. She shyly confided that to him during her first season, not long after the first ball he attended with her. At the time, George only thought it sweet and a touch naive to think that such a love could be found by anyone.

Now, he was not as certain. Did he love Martha enough to spend his life with her? Devoted to her every wish? Anticipating her needs and desires? He thought so. He knew he could provide for her, protect her. George knew he could make her laugh and fill her days with joy.

If only she would let him near enough to plead his case and present his evidence of devotion.

George tossed himself back onto his bed, staring up at the ceiling. If she would not see him, he could at least see her at the concert. Perhaps, after satisfying himself that she was happy without him, he would leave London for the remainder of the season. He only wasted time here, after all, if he refused to go out on the chance he met Martha on the street.

But for now, he would think on the concert and on her beautiful voice. He would hope for her happiness and do his best to ignore his pain.

Chapter Seven

Martha kept her gloved hands firmly clamped around the music for her performance, trying not to crinkle the pages as the carriage bounced quickly down the streets of London. Her mother and father sat across from her, holding hands and speaking quietly about the evening ahead. They were doing their best not to add to her nervousness, only saying kind things about the other young ladies performing, not foisting expectations of a grand exhibition upon her.

She did enough of that on her own. But how could Martha help it when the Calverts were such a well-loved family? She had been to three of their famous Christmas balls now, and even danced with their son at the last holiday gathering. The heir to the family estate and title was a year younger than she, but he had been every inch the gentleman. Her father teased her about that dance for a time, but when Martha would only roll her eyes and ignore the comments, he left off saying a word.

It struck her as strange that no one ever thought to tease her about George. Especially if her feelings for him were obvious enough that her mother noticed them. After all, she danced with George as often as society permitted, usually twice at a ball when there were few gentlemen, and once at every crush.

"It is such a kindness for Lady Annesbury to invite you to sing," her mother said, bringing Martha back to the present. "I know she enjoyed your voice during last year's carols."

"It's nothing extraordinary," Martha said, her gloved fingers tightening on the music sheets again. "I am only grateful you are to accompany me, Mama."

"This is a treat for me," her father said, looking at one and then the other with a smile. "I get to see two of my favorite ladies sharing their most excellent talents."

"And someday, Sarah might be able to perform with us as well."

"Thank heavens you two are far apart in age, and we aren't escorting two young ladies about during the season," her father said, shaking his head at the very thought.

"Sarah has years and years before we have to worry about her. Thomas will be the next problem," her mother said. "That boy is likely to never step more than two feet from a stable, once he reaches his majority."

They all laughed, easing Martha's nervousness. But once that emotion receded, her mind turned of its own accord back to the topic which had been grieving her before: Mr. George Brody. It was likely he would be invited, as his family always came to the country events hosted by the earl and his countess. Would he send his regrets or make an appearance?

While she hoped she might see him, she felt certain he would not come. Why would he, when he managed to avoid her so thoroughly up until now? And it was all her own fault. Her pride had been stung, and she lashed out, hurting her dearest friend. It served her right that he obeyed her wishes.

Their carriage arrived, and they alighted, Mr. Gilbert climbing out first, the better to assist his wife and daughter. "Here we are," he said, "safe and sound, and ready for an evening of the finest entertainment."

Martha smiled at the compliment and followed her parents up the steps to the Calverts' London home. Her nervousness was gone, but in its place loneliness clung.

If only George were here, she thought. He would know precisely how to cheer me up.

His very presence would be enough.

They had arrived early, so as not to make Lady Annesbury anxious about her program. The gracious countess greeted them as if they were all the oldest and dearest of friends.

"Mr. and Mrs. Gilbert, I am absolutely delighted to have you here this evening. Thank you for coming and allowing Miss Gilbert to perform. Dear child," she said before turning to Martha. "You have the voice of an angel. I have arranged for you to sing directly after the Rathingham girls." She leaned a trifle closer, her eyes twinkling merrily. "They are very enthusiastic musicians, so I think the audience will need something a little more soothing after their lively duet."

"Thank you, Lady Annesbury. I will do my best." Martha curtsied.

"Of course, and it will be wonderful." The lady graciously patted Martha on the hand and then turned to great her next guest with kind words and a warm smile.

"She is a lovely woman," Mrs. Gilbert remarked. "She never forgets a name, never speaks ill of anyone, and I always feel at ease in her home."

Mr. Gilbert nodded his agreement and steered the ladies towards some refreshment. "You both had better take something now before the performances begin. Martha, have something warm to drink, for your throat."

"Thank you, Father." She accepted a cup of tea from a server and turned her attention to the house, looking about her with interest. The Calverts were an old family, with roots going back to William the Conqueror, though their nobility and the Annesbury title had only been granted a few generations previous. They had wealth in abundance, but they did not brandish it about the way others in society did.

"Miss Gilbert," a deep voice said from her side. She turned to see the heir presumptive, Lord Lucas Calvert, at her side. "This is a pleasure, seeing someone from home." He bounced a little as he spoke, making his already impressive height more noticeable. "Are you to perform tonight?"

"Yes, I am. What gave me away?"

He nodded to her hand where she still held her music sheets tightly. "I didn't think you carried music around for your own amusement. What will you be presenting?"

"I am singing She Never Told Her Love."

"Ah, an operatic piece. There is a lot of complicated accompaniment, isn't there?" His knowledge of the piece surprised her. It wasn't something she expected a young man to be familiar with.

"Yes, but my mother plays beautifully, and we've been practicing." She put her teacup down and glanced around the room again. "We have rearranged some of the music, too. I will sing it in German and then in English."

"That will be a great treat. And you look just the part for it, covered in roses."

Martha looked down at her dress, a soft pink silk she especially loved, with a lace overlay patterned after a tangle of roses. Small pink buds made from ribbon adorned her hair, and around her throat was yet another rose embellishment. "I suppose I do."

George said she looked lovely in pink, or else he teased her by claiming it the most abhorrent of colors. He knew it was her favorite color. She looked up again, her eyes searching for his dark head above the crowd.

Lucas Calvert followed her eyes around the room. "Are you looking for someone?"

"Oh." Martha felt heat rise up the back of her neck and tried to laugh, hoping to keep it away from her cheeks. "Not at all. I merely wondered how many here I would recognize."

"A fair few, I think. Mother enjoys parties and always strives to fill up the house with guests." He smiled and gestured to a group of ladies. "Shall I introduce you, Miss Gilbert?"

Martha took the young man's arm and tried to distract herself as he made introductions to young ladies in their first and second seasons. Though they could not be far apart in age, she felt much older than they, as they giggled and flirted with the future Earl of Annesbury. He did not seem overcome by their attentions but kept turning the conversation from one young lady to another. If only Martha's skill with conversation was half so perfect.

Though she watched the entry to the ballroom, set up for the concert instead of dancing, Martha did not see George. As the time of the performance drew near, her heart continued to sink. At last, Lady Annesbury brought everyone's attention to the front of the room, where she welcomed all and bid them take their seats, with the performers in the first row of chairs.

After finding her mother, Martha led them to two chairs in the front, and her father sat directly behind them. The performances began with a beautiful concerto, followed by a gentleman playing violin with his sister at the pianoforte, a beautiful instrument imported from Vienna, the absolute latest in design.

The Rathingham sisters took their turn at last, one playing and the other singing what was meant to be a stirring song of battle. But Lady Annesbury had been very kind when she spoke of their eagerness; between them, the young ladies had more enthusiasm than true talent. But they were beautiful and smiled brightly at all, so the audience gave their applause freely.

Mr. Gilbert leaned forward, placing a hand on his daughter's shoulder. "You will do beautifully, Martha."

She raised her hand to cover his, giving it a gentle squeeze. Her gratitude for two loving parents flooded her, and Martha rose with confidence. She placed the music for her mother and then stood, hands folded before her, waiting to sing.

The German did not come easily to her as a spoken language, but when she sang, she knew the words were formed correctly. Martha kept her eyes just above the crowd, projecting her voice to the back of the room, hoping her soprano sounded as rich to her audience as it did to her ears.

She had a special fondness for *Twelfth Night*. She especially liked Viola's character, doing all she could for her true love without being able to reveal herself to him fully. Shakespeare had marvelously written Viola, and Martha now understood the lovelorn woman better than she had before. To love a man and remain unable to confess that love was a terrible position for both of them.

Her mother's talent aided her greatly, presenting a beautiful tapestry of music for her to add the tragic words of Viola to her unsuspecting love. She hoped her mother would be thanked and acknowledged for her part in the piece. Then came the time to sing Haydn's words in English, almost as they were originally written by Shakespeare.

She never told her love,
She never told her love,
But let concealment, like a worm in the bud,

Feed on her damask cheek;

And that was when she saw him, standing at the back of the room, his head above those seated before him. George had come, and now he watched her, his eyes riveted to her form. Her voice faltered as she looked at him, too far back for her to see the expression on his face. Was he upset that he had come and now must see her, singing before everyone? Did he regret their parting as she did?

He took a step forward, lifting his chin, and grinned broadly, as he always did across a crowded room when he caught her looking.

She found her voice, and it was unlikely anyone but her mother noticed she nearly missed her mark.

She sat, like Patience on a monument,

Smiling at grief.

Would he understand when she sang those words that she spoke of herself? Martha loved George with her whole heart, and she had waited years for him to love her back. But how could he know, when she said nothing? Did nothing but smile at his wit and serve him coffee instead of tea?

Smiling, smiling, at grief.

The music trailed away poignantly, the last note echoing in the near silent room, and then there was applause. Martha was not a great musician, but she put her heart into the music, and that made all the difference in a room filled by people intent on her words.

Her eyes stayed on George, standing tall and handsome in the back, his hands clapping. She made her curtsy to the crowd, then she turned to gesture to her mother, who took her curtsy as well. When she looked again, back to where George had stood, he was already gone, taking her heart with him.

Chapter Eight

Martha's parents did not mind in the slightest when she begged to return home early. They both had caught up with the friends they most wished to see, and they had enjoyed accepting compliments on their daughter's lovely voice. Truly, she could not ask for better parents. When she told her mother she felt fatigued, not another word was said on the matter until they were safely ensconced in their carriage.

"Your piece was truly beautiful," her father said across the darkened carriage. "It was far lovelier than any of the times I heard you practice, especially at the end. I did not know whether I would burst with pride or shed tears."

"Thank you, Papa." Martha closed her eyes and tilted her head back against the seat. "I am glad we made you proud."

"My girls always make me proud," he said, his voice sure and strong. "I am only sorry you are not feeling well enough to bask in the praise a little longer. I think everyone in that room wanted to speak to you afterward. Especially the gentlemen."

"Perhaps that is why she needed to leave." Her mother's knowing tone almost made Martha smile. "It is always better to be a woman of mystery."

"Has that been your goal all these years?" Mr. Gilbert teased.

Martha remained silent, listening to their banter. Their friendship and love, their regard for each other, had been her example of what a happy marriage looked like. Her father was good and kind, treating her mother as though she were royalty. And Mrs. Gilbert reciprocated his outpouring of devotion, supporting him and speaking often of how she admired him. Even when they disagreed, which Martha had seen a few times in her life, anger never entered into their conversation. Frustration, perhaps, but never anything which lingered to sour their relationship.

Maybe that is where I went wrong, she thought. Their carriage rolled to a stop in front of their town home. I let myself be angry at George when he hadn't the slightest idea what I was thinking.

She made up her mind to write to him, to ask him to visit. She would apologize, *again*, and this time she would be honest about her feelings with him. At least if he rejected her at that point, she would have no more questions lingering in her mind, like Viola's "worm in the bud."

They entered their home, the butler and a maid waiting to take their cloaks and gloves.

"Mr. Gilbert, there is a guest waiting for you in the study," Norton said.

"A guest?" Her father's eyes widened, and he looked at his wife in bewilderment. "At this time of evening?"

"Yes, sir. I told him you would not be home for hours, but he said he would wait." Norton's eyes darted to Martha, which made her purse her lips. "I suggest Mrs. and Miss Gilbert wait for you in the parlor. Your guest may wish to speak to them, too."

"Who is it, Norton?" Mrs. Gilbert asked, sounding half exasperated.

The butler answered with a perfectly straight face. "I promised not to say."

Mr. Gilbert looked from his wife to his daughter, then back to the butler. "Then I had better see for myself and trust you don't allow assassins to lay in wait for us, Norton."

"Not at all, Mr. Gilbert." Norton half-bowed and then led the way to her father's study.

"How unusual." Mrs. Gilbert shook her head. "Come, Martha. We may as well wait and see what strange turn our night will now take."

Martha followed quietly, wishing she could go up to her room and begin writing her letter to George at once. She had to make things right with him, as soon as possible.

George had gone to the concert uncertain of how long he would stay, or what he would say to any friends he found there. His only goal to see Martha, even if from afar, to determine the state of her happiness. He came late, just as all the guests were gathering in the ballroom-turned-concert-hall, and he waited until nearly everyone had shuffled inside to find their seats before he made his way to the back.

A few other gentlemen were standing, having given up chairs to ladies, and they now stood quietly speaking at the rear of the room. George kept to himself, his eyes searching the front row for Martha. It did not take him long to find the only dark hair with tiny pink embellishments nestled among the curls. Martha's dark hair, nearly black, was piled up to reveal the graceful lines of her neck and shoulders. He would know her form anywhere, even across a crowded room such as this.

He waited through the performances, only listening with half an ear, transfixed by the slight movements she made as she listened and applauded the musicians who came before her.

Then, at last, she stood and made her way to the front of the room. Her mother moved to the piano to accompany her. It was not unheard of for the older generation to entertain at an Annesbury concert, but they usually did not accompany young ladies enjoying a London season. George knew Mrs. Gilbert to be an accomplished musician, and with Martha's lovely voice, their piece would certainly be beautiful.

George recognized the music from Haydn before Martha made it to the second line. During her first season in London, they had gone to the opera together. It was not a night of grand performances, but rather something of a review, in which the talented actors and singers each performed short works for the crowds to build excitement for the rest of the season. They heard Haydn's music there, and Martha had fallen in love with it.

Twelfth Night was her favorite of Shakespeare's plays, where other young maidens demurely suggested *Romeo and Juliet* to be the most brilliant of his romances. George rather preferred stories wherein the principle characters did not die. Martha had teased him about this, telling him he lacked a flare for the dramatic.

Her voice, lifting him to new heights this evening, gave him an understanding of why someone might choose to die for love. Her voice could only be compared to a member of the heavenly choir, her grace, and beauty more enchanting than any great work of art, and when her eyes fell on his, he felt his heart stop, leaving him to enjoy that perfect moment for the rest of time. She must have felt that same longing, for her voice faltered, trembled an instant, and then returned with more determination and passion in each note.

…Smiling at grief.

The words touched his soul, and George knew hope at last.

The moment she made her curtsy, he took himself away, leaving with all possible haste. He did not wish to linger and make polite conversation, nor did he desire to seek her out amid the throngs of people and break the spell she'd placed on him with her song.

George went straightaway to her home, knowing it could be hours before she returned, yet he knew in his heart he would not have long to wait. He would remain there, for an eternity if he must, to have an audience with her.

After he spoke to her father.

Because he was ready to do things the right way with Martha Gilbert.

Norton had been hard to convince, until George confessed his true reason for showing up while the family was out, at such an unheard-of hour. But the butler had known George for years and relented, at last, in allowing him to wait in the study. Finally, Mr. Gilbert came.

George hurried across the room to the older gentleman, not wasting a moment to form proper greetings. "Mr. Gilbert, I must speak to you at once about Miss Gilbert. I wish for your permission to court her, sir. I intend to do all I can to persuade her to be my wife."

Mr. Gilbert, barely in the doorway of the study, extended his hand to George. "It's about time, boy. We'd all but given up on you."

Stunned, George shook the man's hand. "You expected that I would ask…?"

Mr. Gilbert nodded deeply, his eyebrows raising to his hairline. "For some time, yes. But these last few weeks, her mother and I wondered if we were wrong. But you have cared for her so long, and she has been very patiently waiting. Enough. Martha is only in the other room. She should not have to wait any longer. Tell me this, Brody, and I will fetch her for you: do you love her?"

"With all my heart." George did not have to think before he answered and speaking the truth of it aloud filled him with greater confidence than before. "And if she will have me, I will spend the rest of my life making up for the time I've already cost us."

"Good man. You have my blessing, and her mother's. I will send Martha to you, and you will hear what she has to say on the matter." Mr. Gilbert reached out to clap him on the arm before he left his study, not even closing the door behind him.

George walked toward the fire and then turned, watching the doorway, waiting for her. When at last Miss Martha Gilbert stepped into the doorway, light from the hall framing her perfectly, the pink in her gown matching the rosy shade of her cheeks, George wondered that it had taken him so long to see the truth of his feelings for her. He had grown so comfortable with her friendship that he neglected to pay attention to his heart reaching out for hers, finding a perfect match in temperament, spirit, and humor.

"Mr. Brody," she said, her eyes widened and her lips parting. "I did not know it was you waiting. Father said—" She stopped speaking and shook her head, her eyes narrowing instead. "You left the concert early. I did not think to see you this soon."

He took a cautious step forward, watching her expression closely. "I did not wish to share you with a hundred other people present. I came here. To wait."

Martha took a hesitant step forward, her hands clasped before her. "For me, Mr. Brody? After all the horrid things I said to you when last we met? I should not have said them. I did not truly mean to blame you for my unmarried state. That is, I did not wish you gone to make way for suitors." She stopped and bit her bottom lip, her eyes beseeching him to understand what she could not say.

"You ought to have said much more," he said, taking two steps closer this time, his eyes focused on hers. "I have come to realize that I have been a blind, abominable, stupid man. All this time, it has been my fault that you remain unmarried." He shook his head and covered the remaining distance between them, reaching his hands out to her. "Miss Gilbert, my dearest Martha, I took your companionship for granted, and it is only in these last weeks when I knew you might be taken from me forever, that I came to realize how I truly feel for you." He took in a deep breath, searching her face for hope.

"And what did you realize, George?" she whispered, his given name sounding like music when spoken by her.

"I love you," he said, raising both shoulders and spreading his still empty hands in a helpless gesture. "I came to tell you, to ask if I might court you, just the other day. Then you banished me, and I knew I did not deserve you. But tonight, when I heard you sing Viola's lament, I thought I must try once more."

Martha stared up at him, her expression more serene, and she lifted her hands to place them delicately in his. "George, I have waited to hear you say those words. I have loved you so long." Tears sparkled in her eyes and her lips curved upward in a dazzling smile.

"Then allow me to court you, Martha. Please, I must do it properly."

She laughed. "Only if it is a short courtship, my wonderful George. And only if we are married this spring, at home."

George could not allow that enthusiastic comment to pass without an equally exuberant response. He bent down, eyes on hers. “I love you. We will do exactly as you say.”

Her eyes went to his lips, then back up again. Her next words were nearly breathless. “Then I say we will live happily ever after.”

His lips met hers, his arms gathered her closer, and George knew if forever with Martha tasted and felt like this, he would be a happy man for the rest of his days. He would spend those days doing all he could to see his love’s beautiful smile and make the roses bloom in her cheeks.

Author's Notes:

Thank you for reading *Martha's Patience*. I had such fun writing this love story. This novella is part of my Branches of Love series. The first novel in the series, *The Social Tutor*, is available on Amazon.com for purchase as an ebook, audio book, or paperback, and it's in the Kindle Unlimited library. If you enjoyed reading about Martha and George, you'll love seeing Thomas Gilbert all grown up and confronted with the very determined, and incredibly vivacious, Christine Devon.

Keep reading for a sneak peek at the first chapter of *The Social Tutor* and my fairy-tale retelling, *The Captain and Miss Winter*.

Sneak Peek of The Social Tutor

Chapter One

November 1st, 1811

"Waiting on a letter one knows to be full of exciting news is an excruciating experience," Christine Devon said, slumping in her chair in a most unladylike manner.

"Are you waiting for the post again?" asked her younger sister. Rebecca glanced away from her book to offer a teasing smile. "Whatever for?"

"I hope the letter will come today and save us all your anxieties on the matter." Julia, the eldest of the three, did not even look up from her stitching as she commented. This meant she didn't see Christine's glare.

"You ought to try reading, Christine," Rebecca said softly. "The news sheets are here on the table. I know you enjoy them."

"I find it interesting to be aware of what goes on in the world," Christine acknowledged, barely glancing at the papers. "Father says I ought not to read them too much. They are meant for gentlemen."

Julia made a noise which sounded suspiciously like a snort. "He will never know, Christine. If you like them, read them."

Checking out the window once more, Christine darted to the table to snatch the *Times*, a week old now, and went back to her seat.

"There. Now you needn't be so anxious." Rebecca settled more deeply into her chair and lifted her book again. "Reading helps to pass the time, after all."

Christine could barely read a full sentence without looking out the window. She did not want to miss the arrival of the post and could not fully attend to the latest opinion piece on the state of the King's sanity. The proposal of naming the Crown Prince as Regent interested her, she decided she would have to read through the pages again, after the post arrived.

Christine had waited in this manner every day for the last three weeks. Aunt Jacqueline, the widow of an earl, likely did not know how much her niece longed for the missive. The esteemed lady's letter would be positively full of instructions and lists for the coming London Season, because it was at last Christine's turn to make her debut into society. At nineteen, she was on the older side when it came to the hopeful young misses stepping out for the first time, but she felt grateful she was granted a season at all, especially after her sister Julia's spectacular failure four years previously.

Christine did not actually know *what* Julia's spectacular failure consisted of, as no one in the family ever told the whole story outright. All Christine knew of the matter consisted of her father's quiet comments muttered at family dinners, her aunt's vague mention of the "unfortunate affair," and Julia's slow withdrawal from her sisters.

Whatever the past mistake or embarrassment, Christine determined long ago that *her* triumphant season, as one of the most sought-after young women in London, would elevate the family to new heights.

"You ought to stop straining your neck like that, looking out," Rebecca commented, bringing Christine out of her thoughts abruptly. Her younger sister watched from behind her book, dark eyes twinkling merrily. "You might overstretch it and then where would you be? I doubt goose necks are in fashion at the moment."

A small chuckle escaped from Julia, and Christine could not help smiling as well. "We cannot have that, I suppose." She pulled her shoulders up and tucked her chin down against her chest. "Do you think a turtle-like posture more the thing?"

Rebecca pretended to consider, and Christine laughed until Rebecca joined in the merriment. Christine knew her expression mirrored her younger sister's; they looked the most alike of their siblings, taking after their father with their dark, waving hair and brown eyes. Julia looked more like their mother, her hair a lighter shade of brown and her eyes flecked with copper. Their younger brother, away at school, had light, curly hair and dark brown eyes. Only when they all stood together did they look related.

Christine often wished she looked more like their late mother, if only to feel closer to her.

Their mother passed when Christine was fourteen years old, leaving it to their father's elder sister to turn the sisters out in style for the season. Aunt Jacqueline took charge of sponsoring her into society and chaperoning her to all the important events, with her father paying the bills for the modiste, seamstress, millinery, and whatever else deemed necessary. After all, as he said time and again, a woman's first season was an investment for the whole family.

At last she saw the footman assigned to retrieve the mail. He fetched it from the inn, where the mail coach stopped twice a day. The poor young man always came the long way around the house to avoid the smells of the stables. Apparently, he had an aversion to horses.

Christine could hardly imagine anything more tragic than to be deprived of horses and daily rides for something as absurd as a damp nose.

Christine hurried from the morning room and across the whole house, choosing to take the servants' stair instead of the main staircase in order to catch the young man more quickly. Today simply had to be the day that Aunt Jacqueline's letter came. They needed to plan for the season ahead, and it was already November.

Mr. Devon planned to remove the family to London immediately following the Earl of Annesbury's annual Christmas ball. That left Christine precious little time to prepare herself for a grand entrance into society.

She flew into the kitchen at the same moment the footman entered and nearly dove at him to retrieve the post.

The startled servant jumped backward as she snatched the letters from his hands. She clutched at the two envelopes and looked at their direction with great anxiety. The first was to their father in a hand she thought to belong to their solicitor, the second was addressed to her.

"Ah, Miss Christine." The butler greeted her dryly from his place at the table. She blushed as she looked at him but made no apologies. She ought to have waited for him to bring the post to Julia.

"I'll take mine now, thank you." Christine tossed the unwanted letter back to the footman without looking and dashed out of the kitchen as fast as she could, going to the garden. She hardly noticed the chill in the air, and thankfully already wore one of Julia's knitted shawls.

She stopped at the first sun-warmed bench she came to, sat, and tore the seal on the letter with abandon, nearly wrinkling the paper in her haste.

My Dearest Niece,

It is with great pleasure that I write to assure you of my determination to sponsor you this season. While it is no secret that I dearly wish to give you this opportunity, your father expressed concern when last we spoke that you might lack another year of experience before entering society. I reminded him that nineteen is more stylish an age and sounds better than twenty to future beaux. If we wait until you are twenty, people will wonder why we have been hiding you. I daresay most have forgotten about Julia's unfortunate season, but there is no reason to dredge up curiosity in any who recall those events...

Her aunt went on to give a detailed list of Christine's needed purchases before her arrival in town, and made a suggestion as to colors and styles that a country seamstress might be able to employ to advantage. The bulk of the shopping would be done upon her arrival in London with her father.

Christine clutched the letter to her chest, her elation filling her with hope until she knew she must glow. At last, her season! Her chance to prove to her father that she was worthy of his affection, worthy of his pride. Her chance to step onto the stage of the world and make a match of such societal importance that other debutantes would positively wilt in comparison. Her match would be brilliant. She hoped for a title, and certainly for wealth, and to give her father contacts in the upper echelons of society, thus ensuring her family's success in the years and even generations to come.

While her father, and indeed the whole family, benefited from his sister's marriage into the *ton*, he remained on the fringes, an untitled gentleman with business interests shared by several more noble property owners.

Christine sailed back into the morning room to share the wonderful news. Julia sat in her favorite chair still stitching something in a terribly practical shade of gray, likely for one of their tenants. Rebecca was engaged with her novel once more.

Pausing in her step, Christine looked over the scene with a smile. She loved days like this, where they sat together quietly, enjoying each other's company. Horace, the baby of the family and their father's heir, had been away too long. She wondered what he would be doing, were he present. He certainly would not be sitting as quietly as Rebecca, tucked into her chair like a kitten curled in a basket.

She decided to interrupt the quiet, making her announcement cheerfully. "Aunt Jacqueline has written at last."

Rebecca looked up from her page with a smile. "Oh Christine, how wonderful for you."

Julia raised her eyebrows, not even pausing in her work.

Christine stared at her elder sister, perplexed by the complete lack of attention. "I am very excited," she added, still enthusiastic. "She has given me a list of things to purchase before we remove to London."

Julia nodded and this time deigned to speak. "If you will write it out for me, I will make an estimation on the expense for Father to look over."

Rebecca closed her book and stood, coming to peer at the letter over Christine's shoulder. Rebecca and Christine stood near enough in height, making the maneuver easy on the younger sister.

"What else does Aunt say? Does she tell you what to expect when you make your curtsy?"

Highly irritated by Julia's lack of enthusiasm, Christine deliberately turned her full attention to her sixteen-year-old sister. "She does. She writes all about it; the dress I will wear and who will make it for me, the ceremony at court. She has included the most wonderful itinerary, though a great deal will depend upon the invitations we receive after we arrive in town."

"I am happy for you." Rebecca looked from Christine to Julia and her smile faltered. "Aren't you happy for her, Julia?"

"Certainly." Julia's fingers nimbly moved the needle up and down, still not looking up. "Christine has been dreaming of this for years."

"Ever since your season," Christine said, lifting her chin. An errant curl fell out of its pin at that moment, spoiling the effect of her now perfect posture. "Four years of dreaming."

Julia paused and glanced up, her staid expression never betraying her thoughts. "A long time indeed. I hope all that dreaming won't spoil the reality for you."

Christine narrowed her eyes at her elder sister, disappointed with Julia's indifference at a time like this. She didn't even feign excitement for Christine's opportunity. "As long as I end the season with a husband of means, I do not think it will be at all spoiled."

Julia shrugged and went back to her sewing, as though completely unconcerned. "If that is your goal, you are likely right. Be careful, Christine."

Christine raised her eyebrows. "Careful of what? Repeating your missteps?"

For a brief moment, Julia's posture stiffened. Christine dared to think she rattled her sister enough, at last, to find out what those missteps had been.

Julia, ever the master of her emotions, regained her poise.

"Father is an exacting person. He will expect perfection and, as a mortal being, you will fall short of that. I have no doubt you will do your best, but if you hope to gain his approval by marrying correctly, I am afraid you will be disappointed. His expectations will grow with whatever consequence a good marriage would bring you." Julia kept her eyes on the work in her hands, her words falling almost carelessly from her lips.

Hardly believing her sister uttered so many words regarding a topic she normally avoided, it took Christine a short space of time to recover her thoughts. "I do not think it is as impossible as you make it seem. I will succeed in a way that makes Father proud. In fact, I will exceed his expectations." She nodded smartly.

"I suppose nineteen is so much more mature than seventeen," Julia said lightly. "When I attempted to do the same."

"Precisely why Father made me wait those extra two years," Christine stated, crossing her arms before her. "Greater maturity of thought. A better understanding of his wishes."

Julia shrugged, her disinterest in the conversation clearly expressed by her lack of attentiveness. "Certainly. I do wish to caution you. Father's ambitions for you may not be entirely what *you* expect. Be careful."

While Christine loved Julia dearly, there were moments when she wished to throttle her sister for ruining things for the rest of them.

Rebecca interjected with an overly bright tone. “Will you write Aunt back today?” Christine had nearly forgotten her younger sister was present, which happened with greater frequency of late.

Christine ignored her younger sister and took a step toward Julia. “Careful of what, Julia? What sage advice have you to offer, considering the lack of success during your season in London?”

Julia’s eyes snapped up and narrowed. “My lack of success, as you call it, happened for a reason. I hope you take care that our father’s goals do not overshadow your happiness, Christine.”

“Our father’s goals are the same as any other father’s when a daughter comes of age,” Christine argued, clenching the hand not holding the letter. “We should consider and respect his wishes in this matter, as dutiful children.”

Rebecca darted forward, between them, clearly sensing Christine’s prickly feelings on the subject. “We do respect Father. I think Julia meant that she wants you to be happy with the choice you make this season. That is all. Julia? Isn’t that what you meant?”

Julia rose, lifting her sewing basket with her. “Yes. Exactly that. I hope your choice makes you happy.” As she moved to leave the room she added, in a most unconcerned manner, “If you are given any choices, that is. Receiving an offer is never a certain thing.” Without another word she swept out the door.

"Why does she do that?" Christine asked, glaring at the empty doorway. "Why can she not be happy for me?"

"Her season *was* a failure, Christine," Rebecca said softly. "I think it hurts her to be reminded of it. Father brings it up so often."

"If she would tell us what happened, we could be more sympathetic to her," Christine huffed, folding her arms across her waist. "Instead, we are left to guess, and she refuses to say a word unless to offer dire warnings."

Rebecca laughed, though it sounded strained. "She loves us, Christine. Julia wants us to do well. So we do not end up as she has."

"A spinster."

"That is not kind," Rebecca said more softly. "She is our sister."

Christine barely refrained from saying more on the subject. Though she may regret her words later, at the moment she wished for someone to be happy for *her*. She thrust the letter out to Rebecca, trying to regain her former excitement. "Here. Read Aunt Jacqueline's letter. I must make a list for Julia."

Christine left the room, determined to do all in her power to avoid Julia's fate of spinsterhood and disappointment.

Sneak Peek of *The Captain and Miss Winter*

Chapter One

February 1816

Once upon a time, Caspar Graysmark had thought a career in the military would be precisely everything he wanted. That was before he actually joined the British army, before he'd marched through the war-torn countries of Europe, living in the dirt and subsisting on rations of moldy bread and wilted cabbages.

Freezing rain came down in sheets, and he could see nothing before or behind him in the bare-branched forest. The night remained black and cold. He was lost, somewhere near the Franco-Spanish border, in the mountains east of Larrau, a village small enough it shouldn't even be on the map. A village he only knew to look for because he had been through it once before, leading a small company of men on a secret assignment.

And I'm just as lost now as I was then.

He'd supposed that going to battle would be something he'd take to naturally, after all his years of playing soldier about his father's estate. But marching up and down the garden walk with his brothers was nothing like firing into a line of living, breathing men.

After Napoleon's surrender, Caspar had intended to go home to England and never leave its shores again. Except, as he explained in a letter to his mother, he had to perform one last task. One last deed that weighed upon him. His honor demanded he see it through.

Caspar shuddered and pulled his heavy fur coat closer about himself, then dismounted to lead his horse, Fortinbras. Perhaps on foot he would do a better job of navigating.

Ice crystals crunched beneath his feet, and the sleet turned to snow. If he didn't find shelter in short order, Caspar had little hope of him and his horse surviving until the next morning.

A flicker in the distance, between the dark trees, caught his weary gaze.

"Light," he whispered aloud. His horse snorted. "There's a light." He almost chuckled. Talking to his horse the past few days had become his only opportunity to hear his own voice in the wilds of hill and forest. He led the animal forward, his progress as slow as before but now more hopeful.

Down the other side of a hill he went, narrowly avoiding tree branches, his eyes fixed ahead on a small square of glowing orange.

He stepped out of the trees into a flat, clear space of land, yards away from the welcoming light. It had to be a window. It *had* to be a window. His mind wouldn't play such tricks on him.

His eyes took in more as he drew closer. It was a small stone house, a cottage. He kept moving, all the way to the window, his teeth chattering and bits of ice frozen to his beard and eyebrows.

Caspar didn't look through the window, only made for the door.

He knocked with the hand not holding his horse, then waited. Good breeding alone kept him from simply rushing inside to the source of warmth and brightness.

~

Scarlett's head jerked up from where it had rested on her sister's shoulder. Blanche sat upright, sucking in a sharp breath.

"Someone knocked," Blanche whispered, her wide eyes on the door. The orange tabby in her lap jumped down to hide beneath the bench.

"Who would be out in weather like this?" their grandmother asked, lowering her knitting needles. Her white eyebrows drew together. She met Scarlett's eyes. "Answer it, child."

Blanche remained where she sat, cautious and unwilling to act hastily, as always, and grandmother's old bones would ache too much if she moved far from the fire. It fell to Scarlett as the elder sister, as it usually did, to undertake a difficult task.

She stood, dropping her half of the blanket back onto the old bench. Adjusting her tattered shawl about her shoulders, she went across the room to the door.

She ought to ask who stood on the other side, given that the only thing protecting her from the elements, beasts, and less-than-savory men was the very door knocked upon. But truly, it wasn't the sturdiest of doors. If it was pushed hard enough, the bolt wouldn't even hold.

Scarlett tilted her chin upward and slid the bolt open, then swung the door open with all the confidence she could muster. Cold night air rushed inside, slipping around her feet to find the corners of their tiny cottage, like cats coming in from the weather. Scarlett hardly noticed, once she saw his eyes.

A giant of a man stood at their threshold, his striking blue eyes the only light thing about him. He was robed in dark furs, his face covered in a short beard, a hat low upon his brow. He was a head taller than she and at least twice as wide in his shoulders. She should've been frightened of him, and would've been, if not for those eyes.

He spoke in broken French, his voice deep and rumbling. "*S'il vous plaît. J'ai besoin d'un abri.*"

Her grandmother called to her in English. "Who is it, my flower?"

"A man," Scarlett answered, her voice only a whisper. She cleared her throat and raised her voice, though her eyes never left his face. "A man, asking for shelter."

"If he means us no harm, you had better let him inside."

Scarlett looked from his piercing gaze down to his stout boots and back up.

The man shook his head, his expression turning confused. "You speak English?" When was the last time she'd heard a man's voice speak her native tongue? Not since her father's death.

"We do." She stood on her toes to peer over his shoulder, seeing only a horse behind him. "If you wish for shelter here, you must give me your word you mean us no harm."

He nodded quickly. "On my honor, I wish no one in this house ill will, and more, I will do whatever is in my power to repay your kindness."

His manner of speech was cultured, and his tone low enough to make her feel its charm all the way through her bones. She shivered, and not from the cool air filling the space between them. "Very well. There is a shed against the cottage, just there." She pointed to the left of the door. "It's big enough for your horse. Put him there and then come back. We will give you shelter."

The man, despite his shivering, actually bowed to her. She could not remember the last time she'd been shown such courtesy. She closed the door, then rushed back the seven steps to the hearth, a blush warming her cheeks.

Their cottage only held two rooms; their sleeping chamber and the room they sat in made up the whole of the cottage. They had carpets that were not more than woven rags, a table with broken and mismatched chairs, and the bench she and her sister had covered with an old quilt and stuffed straw cushions. It was clean and tidy, but the floor was hard-packed earth, and all cooking was done over the same fire that kept them warm.

"He's coming in after he takes care of his horse," she announced to her sister and grandmother, as though they hadn't heard every word of the exchange between herself and the stranger. "What can we give him?"

Blanche rose and went to their hutch near the table, which acted as their pantry and larder both. She opened the cabinet and took out a wrapped loaf of bread and a jar of boiled chicken. "He can begin with bread, and we will add the chicken to our stew."

"A wise idea," their grandmother said. The stew pot hung on a hook they could swing in and out of the fire. "We'll warm his insides as best we can. What a night to be out wandering in the woods!"

Scarlett went back to the door, listening for the stranger's return and watching her sister hurry to add chicken to the cooling pot, which had only contained carrots, cabbage, and a smattering of spices before.

She didn't question helping the stranger. Not on a night like this. Not after looking into his eyes.

Even if he was a thief, they had little enough to steal. Their clothes were worn thin, their precious things had long since been sold or bartered away; all they truly had left was each other.

She heard the crunch of footsteps outside the door and opened it, standing aside to allow the large man entry. Though she knew their cottage to be small, it had never felt as tiny as it did when he stepped inside. The man filled the very air they breathed.

Scarlett closed and bolted the door behind him.

"Thank you," he said, the words clipped from between his chattering teeth. "You have saved me."

Scarlett bit her bottom lip, looking to her grandmother for guidance.

"Come in, sir. Come and share our fire. Scarlett, take his coat," Grandmother instructed, not moving from her place by the hearth. Blanche stood behind Grandmother, her fingers gripping the back of their grandmother's chair.

The man bowed to them, then started to slip his arms free of the great fur coat on his back. Scarlett hurried to help him, taking the shoulders of the garment in her hands, catching it before it hit the floor. The fur was soaked through, nearly frozen, and weighed more than Scarlett expected. Barely keeping hold of it, she went to the table and laid the coat flat upon it. The frost glittered as it melted.

Her eyes went to the man, his back to her. He knelt in front of the fire, holding his hands out to the flame. His whole body still trembled from the cold.

Scarlett looked to Blanche, who met her eyes.

"Quilts," Scarlett said. Her sister nodded and disappeared into their bedroom.

"Sir," Scarlett said, coming near him. "Please, sit, let us take off your boots."

He didn't move to the bench, but sat down on the rug, not moving from the fire even an inch. He stretched his legs out before him, but before he could reach for his boots, Scarlett gripped the heel of one in her hands. She pulled, tugged, and got the large footwear off. She set it by the hearth and began work on the other.

His breeches were long and appeared to be well made. Not the apparel of a trapper or peasant. The man stripped off his gloves, not protesting her help.

Blanche returned, two quilts in her arms.

"Take off the rest of your wet things, young man," Grandmother said, her voice authoritative. "Then we can get you warm."

Young man? Scarlett's eyes raised from the boot in her hands up to his face. His bright blue eyes met hers. How could Grandmother tell? The dark brown beard he wore concealed most of his features.

"Yes, madam," he said, his deep voice rumbling through the small room. It was a pleasant voice, a soothing one.

He took off his hat, then the second coat he wore, and even his socks, all while sitting on their rug before the fire. While it should've been the most inelegant thing Scarlett had ever seen a man do, she found herself examining his broad shoulders, his strong fingers. He met her eyes after he draped his socks across the stones near the fire, and she realized she had been staring, holding his boot, kneeling not a foot away from him the whole time.

Scarlett's cheeks warmed. She moved backward, dropping the boot on the floor, and stood.

Blanche came forward with the quilts, her steps slow and eyes wary, bending to hand them both to the stranger.

The man thanked her, his voice quieter. He wrapped one quilt around his shoulders and laid the other over his lap, bundling himself up. His body had stopped quaking, his teeth no longer clacked together, and he looked about with some curiosity.

"Tell me," he said, looking from Scarlett to Grandmother. "How did three Englishwomen come to live in the middle of a French forest?"

To read this re-telling of the Grimms' Brother's tale, go to Amazon.com and search for ***The Captain and Miss Winter.***

About the Author

Sally Britton lives in the desert with her husband, four children, and a two rescue dogs. She started writing her first story when she was fourteen years old. Reading her way through Jane Austen, Louisa May Alcott, and Lucy Maud Montgomery, Sally determined she wanted to write about the elegant, complex world of centuries past.

Sally graduated from Brigham Young University in 2007 with a bachelor's in English. She met and married her husband not long after and they've been building their happily ever after since that day.

Vincent Van Gogh said, "What is done in love is done well." Sally has taken that as her motto, for herself and her characters, writing stories where love is a choice each person must make, and then go forward with hope to obtain their happily ever after.

All of Sally's published works are available on Amazon.com.

Made in United States
North Haven, CT
08 July 2022